Dearest Mandy

Letters from a Grieving Mother

Carol Albrecht

From
HEARTACHE
To Healing

Northwestern Publishing House
Milwaukee, Wisconsin

Cover photos: ShutterStock, Inc.
Art Director: Karen Knutson
Designer: Pamela Dunn

Library of Congress Control Number: 2005925272
Northwestern Publishing House
1250 N. 113th St., Milwaukee, WI 53226-3284
www.nph.net
© 2007 by Northwestern Publishing House
Published 2007
Printed in the United States of America
ISBN 978 0-8100-1748-1

Contents

Prologue

It was the fullness in her breasts that woke Carrie with a start. What time was it anyway? She turned over and glanced at the glowing digital clock on the dresser. David gave a fitful snore and pulled the covers tighter around him. Four o'clock! Why hadn't the baby awakened yet? Perhaps she was as tired as Carrie tonight. Poor Mandy! All week she'd had the sniffles. At night her little nose got plugged and woke her more than usual. Carrie was exhausted from comforting and nursing her every few hours.

Still, Carrie was surprised that her motherly instinct hadn't kicked in, dragging her from sleep as it usually did, even if Mandy didn't cry. She slipped out of bed and padded down the dark hallway to the nursery. She listened at the doorway for Mandy's labored breathing, but no sound came from the quiet room. A quickening fear gripped her heart as she entered the room. As her eyes grew accustomed to the darkness, she saw Mandy's form in the crib, not in the middle where she'd laid her on her back, but over in the corner. The blanket formed a small dark mound below her.

Carrie never turned on the light at night, but this time, her fingers trembling, she reached for the knob on the Noah's ark lamp on the small, white dresser. A soft glow flooded the room, and Carrie walked slowly, hesitantly, to the baby bed. Mandy lay partly on her left side, her arms flailed out, her usually curled fingers open. Carrie gasped. On the sheet beside the baby were dark spots of blood. Drops of foamy redness still hung on Mandy's bluish lips, her golden curls glistening on her forehead in the shadowy light. Carrie reached out with a shaking hand and touched Mandy's arm. The skin that had been soft and velvety and vibrant when she'd laid her down was now cold and ashen.

Carrie screamed, the sound so terrifying that it bolted David out of his dream and hurled him into the nursery. Carrie clenched the bed slats, her knuckles white. She kept on screaming. Grief and pain and disbelief flooded the air with an unearthly din until at last it ebbed into a low, mournful wail. Carrie's fingers loosened on the slats, and she slipped into a heap on the floor, her anguish momentarily drowned in a blessed sea of nothingness.

Dearest Mandy,

Where do I begin? What do I say? It's been over a
year since you left, yet your memory fills every moment
of my endless days. At night when the house is still, your
spirit surrounds me in the blackness. I reach out to touch
you, and you are gone, gliding away into ghostly shadows.
I sit in the old wooden rocker where Great-grandma rocked
her babies, where Grandma rocked me, and where I rocked
you. My heart is stone; my longing arms, heavy with
emptiness. Now it is not your cries that disturb the night,
but mine. Yours were loud, demanding. Mine are quiet
and deep. Perhaps writing to you will help me heal, if
there is any healing for my shriveled soul.

Tuesday, November 2

Dearest Mandy,

I am so tired. I cannot sleep at night, and I cannot
function in the day. I walk through the hours like a robot.
Daddy says I should see a counselor. How can a counselor
help? Can a counselor bring you back? Can a counselor
make me forget?

I ask, "Why?" and God doesn't answer. He is as silent
as death, as still as the grave. What did I do to deserve this?
What horrible, unspeakable thing did I do to so displease
him? Did I love you too much? Was that my sin? Oh, if
only God would answer! If only he would tell me why!

Dearest Mandy,

It's cold today, so cold that it almost equals the icy numbness in my soul. The wind is pushing its chilly fingers through the door cracks and rattling every window in this old house. It's a day that promises a long winter.

I used to worry on days like this. I worried that Daddy and I couldn't keep it warm enough in your little nursery with the ill-fitting window. I teased that the woolly lambs scampering across your crib sheet at least had fluffy coats to cuddle them. On those last October nights before you left, I zipped you into the fuzzy sleeper bag that my best friend Stacey gave you for a baby gift. You looked like a little wooly lamb yourself snuggled into that cozy white softness. Perhaps I kept you too warm, too protected. As it was, the shivering winds of winter never touched you. I didn't know then that you would leave before you saw your first snowflake, that all you would take from life was sunshine and warmth and flowers to tickle your tiny pink nose.

Oh, Mandy, my Mandy, why did you go? Why did you leave me? Why?

Dearest Mandy,

It's hard for me to write today. Every room I enter is filled with you. I see you as you'd be today, a one-year-old, crawling down the long hallway, searching for me. You'd peek around the corner, looking for me, needing me. I spy you in the nursery, jabbering in your bed, calling me with words only you can understand. I reach out and find just an echo of what might have been. I cannot bear it. I am a shell, a lonely, empty coffin of a life.

Dearest Mandy,

Where is God? I still go to church, but it's been a long time since I've talked with him, heart to heart. I feel as though God betrayed me, giving you to Daddy and me after we had waited so long and then snatching you away. I don't know if I'll ever be the trusting, innocent Christian I once was. Members of our church invite me to activities, but I don't want to go. I haven't been very active since Daddy and I married; I was just too busy teaching school, trying to run the house, being a mom. If God took you away so I'd get busy in church, it didn't work. I don't care about anything there anymore. I first have to find out where I am with God before I can be comfortable in his house. Oh, Daddy and I still go every Sunday, but I feel like a hypocrite, an outsider. All those people sit there thinking God loves them, not knowing that in one second he can destroy their lives.

Dearest Mandy,

Remember how I talked to you yesterday about God? Well, after I finished writing, I thought I would read my Bible, almost as though I were daring God to give me answers. I opened it, and there in front of me was Psalm 121. The first two verses say: "Where does my help come from? My help comes from the LORD, the Maker of heaven and earth." The rest of the psalm tells how God takes care of us. It says that he really cares. Oh, Mandy, I cried when I read that. I guess deep down I want so much to believe that God still loves me and isn't punishing me.

I feel like I'm barely hanging on to faith. I remember years ago in my youth group discussing the passage about "bruised reeds" and "smoldering wicks." That's what I am right now—a bruised reed and a smoldering wick. Will I ever have a bright flame of faith in my soul?

Sunday, November 7

Dearest Mandy,

I went to church today and tried to listen, really listen. The sermon was about forgiveness, and I bit my tongue so I wouldn't cry. Daddy gets upset when I'm weepy all the time. All I could think of was how hard it is for me to forgive God; almost as hard as it is to forgive myself. The funny thing is that I don't even know what to forgive myself for. I don't know what I did wrong to make you die so suddenly. The death certificate said "SIDS," but inside I carry this huge heartache of guilt. Should I have taken you to the doctor sooner? Would that have made a difference? If I had awakened earlier, could I have saved you? Were you too warm, too cold? I don't know; I just don't know.

Monday, November 8

Dearest Mandy,

It's Monday again, and it's raining—a quiet, dreary, all-day kind of rain. I used to love days like this. I could curl up with a good book and wile away the day. Now the rain makes me even sadder, if that's possible. I imagine the raindrops are the tears of angels, mourning with me that you went home much too soon.

4

Dearest Mandy,

Where does Daddy get his strength? He was so good about picking up the pieces and moving on. I wonder if his tears are buried somewhere deep inside where even I can't reach. He loved you so much. He called you Tickle Toes and Tinkerbell and Princess. I watched him snuggle you close and stroke your soft cheek. Where did he put his joy? Mine runs out in tears and pain, but his seems to have vanished, put away as easily as decorations after the party's over. I wonder what he feels inside, how he can jump back into life so easily when all I feel is death. We used to be close, but there's a chasm between us now. We never talk anymore. I can't pretend that losing you doesn't matter, like he can.

Dearest Mandy,

New neighbors moved in today. It looks like an older couple. I never really knew the other people who lived in that small Victorian house, since they kept to themselves. Now I'm the one who doesn't want to see anyone. I suppose Daddy will say we must be neighborly and get acquainted. I don't want to get acquainted. Getting acquainted means asking questions, and people always ask the one I can't bear to hear: "Do you have any children?"

What do I answer? "Yes, but God, who's supposed to love us, took her away." Then they'll be uncomfortable or full of pity, and I'll want to run and hide. Or they'll say something stupid, like "You're young, dear, you can always have more children." Would you believe one woman at church actually said that to me only a week after you died? What did she think you were—a commodity, a disposable piece of humanity? I wanted to scream at her, shriek out that no child could replace you, that you were real and special and loved. I wanted to tell her that I carried you for nine months, felt you kick inside me, sang to you, whispered your name even before you were born.

No, Mandy, I don't need to "get acquainted" with the neighbors.

Thursday, November 11

Dearest Mandy,

Daddy thought I should make some cookies and take them next door. How can I tell him that just getting a meal on the table every night consumes every bit of strength I have? I said I'd try, and he gave me one of his I'm-tired-of-your-grieving looks. I wish I could sit down and really talk to him, tell him that I'm tired of grieving too, but nothing I do seems to help. Oh, I do like writing to you, my little one, and for a few moments it helps to think that you're still near. But then I go back to real life and all the pain washes over me again. You and God and Daddy disappear into that cold, unyielding darkness called my life.

Friday, November 12

Dearest Mandy,

Guess what? I actually baked cookies today! Not that it was easy, but I made myself do it. Maybe if Daddy sees I'm trying, things will get better between us. I want him to love me the way he used to. I want him to hold me and kiss me and tell me I'm the light of his life. Trouble is, the light's burned out in me, so I can't light up either his life or mine. There is a sadness about Daddy too—a weariness in his eyes that wasn't there before. Did I put it there, or did your leaving? Maybe it's a little of both.

Saturday, November 13

Dearest Mandy,

Today is Saturday, so Daddy's home from school. He works hard at teaching and needs the weekends to unwind. Daddy was pleased that I baked cookies for our neighbors. He was especially happy that I made extras since chocolate chip is his favorite.

I don't have much time to write today. After what I said Wednesday, can you believe that I actually offered to go over with Daddy and meet our neighbors? I am trying! They're out in the yard right now, working to get two month's worth of leaves raked up. I'm sure they'll welcome a cookie break. Oh, how I pray they don't ask "the question." I'll be back to tell you all about them tomorrow, my sweet.

Sunday, November 14

Dearest Mandy,

Our new neighbors are nice. They stopped raking as soon as we came and invited us into their half-unpacked kitchen for coffee. They shared the cookies I'd brought, and Daddy found one thing he has in common with Stan (Mr. Tomelson). They both love chocolate chip cookies!

Peg has thick gray hair that wisps around her face. Her eyes are sparkly blue, like yours, and she wears thin, metal-rimmed glasses. She's a tiny lady, filled with energy. She gave me a big hug for the cookies, and it actually felt good. I guess I've been living in my own untouchable shell too long.

And we didn't talk about family at all, thank goodness. We did discover that the Tomelsons will be going to our church; they looked for a church home before they decided to retire here. They went to late service today, so we didn't see them. Daddy told them we could go together next Sunday; then they wouldn't feel so alone. They seemed happy about that. In fact, Peg seems happy about everything. I bet she's never had a tragedy in her life. I wish I could be that joyous, that much in love with living.

Monday, November 15

Dearest Mandy,

Grandma Jurgens called today and invited Daddy and me for Thanksgiving. It'll be nice to get away, I think. Sometimes it seems like there's no pleasing me. I get lonely sitting home all the time, but I'm scared to be with people too. I just don't trust myself. Sometimes I do fine, and sometimes I can barely keep from crying. Grandma did tell me (more like warned me) that her niece Amy and her husband, Alan, would be there too with their two-year-old, Dillon. Even though Grandma never mentions you, she's always worried about hurting me. I wish she would talk about you and not act as though you never existed. Grandpa, that jolly bear of a man, does talk about you. He ignores Grandma's "looks" and says every time we see him, "I sure do miss that little shaver." Isn't it strange? That doesn't hurt me as much as Grandma's ignoring you.

Dearest Mandy,

Daddy was excited about spending Thanksgiving with his mom and dad. I know he wanted his brother Jeff to be there too, but it's such a far trip for him and his wife, Betina, when Jeff only has that day off. I didn't tell Daddy I was relieved they weren't coming. I know I'd be flooded with memories when I saw Betina pregnant, memories of the joy of carrying you, memories of the hopes and dreams we had for you. And, yes, I'd be jealous too. Daddy says I have to ask Betina soon if she wants to use any of your things. The nursery is still there. I can't bear to put away your crib, your changing table, the rainbow-colored fish mobile. How you kicked your legs and squealed with delight when you spied it! The striped pink and white afghan Nana knit for you still hangs over the crib railing, and the neon pink teddy bear Uncle Steve brought stands silent guard in the corner of your bed.

Oh, Mandy, I miss you so much! I can't write anymore . . .

Dearest Mandy,

After I finished writing yesterday, I went into your room. I tried to remember how you looked when you woke up from a nap—all smiley and cooing. It scares me sometimes, because it gets harder and harder to remember what you looked like. Once in a while I even have to stand in front of your picture on the big bookshelf in the living room and absorb your golden curls, your smile, the dancing light in your sky-blue eyes. I inhale, smelling again the sweet smell of baby lotion and delicate shampoo on your shining hair. I feel your soft skin and the downiness of the new fuzz sprouting above your chubby neck. I knew you'd have gorgeous ringlets by the time you were one.

And then that other horrible, frightening picture crowds out the happiness. I see you lying there, stiff and cold, blood on your lips. That memory returns easily. Overwhelms me. Haunts my dreams.

I ran from the nursery and slammed the door. How can I pack your things for Aunt Betina when your life and death call to me from everything you touched?

Thursday, November 18

Dearest Mandy,

Peg came over this morning. She brought a cinnamon coffee cake perched on the plate that I'd had the cookies on. "When a friend brings food, it's only polite to return food on the friendship plate," she announced. "At least that's what my grandma always said."

I'd never heard that before, but I appreciated her kindness. I made coffee, and we sat in the kitchen with the chilly November sun smiling in the window, dappling the red-checked tablecloth you always tried to pull if you were able to get your little hands too close. It was hard for me to make conversation, and I worried that Peg wouldn't like me and would never come back. It's difficult to focus, to make small talk. I used to chatter away. Now it's like all of me has slowed down and I have to think, think, think before the right words come.

Peg didn't seem to notice. She talked about decorating the house, and she talked about God. She told me she couldn't get through a day without God to lean on, that his love had gotten her through a lot of difficult times. I wanted to ask her, "What difficult times have you had?"

but then she might ask if I'd ever gone through anything difficult, and I wasn't ready to share you.

Peg did ask if I had a job. I told her I used to teach first grade, but now I just stayed home. I know it sounded stupid, but Peg never pried. I like her. She doesn't ask the hurting kinds of questions.

Friday, November 19

Dearest Mandy,

I'm sitting here at the kitchen table, writing to you. Outside the leaves are swirling down in blustery gusts of wind. Winter is definitely coming. I keep thinking it should be better for me this year. After all, I made it through Thanksgiving and Christmas and Easter without you last year, although each holiday was a struggle. But, somehow, it seems just as difficult this year. I dread the holidays. Nana had already sent a darling, red velvet Christmas dress by the first of October last year. She just couldn't wait. Instead of wearing it for Christmas, we buried you in it.

Saturday, November 20

Dearest Mandy,

Daddy cleaned out the garage today. I don't know how he stood it out there, since I'm shivering even in the house. I saw him tinkering with the snowblower, getting ready for winter. He never was a last-minute person. I made him hot chocolate. He smiled at that, and I smiled back. I guess it wasn't the right kind of smile because Daddy asked, "When are you going to get on with life and be really happy again? She's not coming back, Carrie. Face it. Get over it. Grow up." My smile broke into pieces, and I went crying from the room.

Dearest Mandy,

Peg and Stan went to church with us today. Pastor spoke about the love of God compelling us to do his work. I felt guilty. I'm not doing anything for God or Daddy or myself. It's like I'm stuck in a time warp, like everything stopped the night of October 25. I don't even know who God is . . . or who Daddy is . . . or even who I am anymore.

Daddy introduced Peg and Stan to some of the members. One older lady, whom I hardly know, whispered loudly to Peg, "You take good care of that young lady. She's had a bad time." Peg raised her eyebrows quizzically at me but didn't say a word. I blushed and turned away. I feel like such a child with everyone wringing their collective hands over me. And yet, I know I'm acting like a child. Somewhere, somehow, there must be healing. If God is God, he must see me and know my pain. Even if I don't know him anymore, maybe he still knows me.

Monday, November 22

Dearest Mandy,

Peg came over today. I was glad to see her, and yet I wasn't. I do like Peg, but I was worried that she'd ask me what that lady meant when she said I'd had a "bad time." I just can't bring myself to tell Peg about you yet. So many people have said the wrong things that I'm afraid to risk sharing you. I want Peg to be my friend, and it'll all be destroyed if she doesn't understand how much you meant to me.

Peg needed some scissors. Hers, she said, were buried in any one of a hundred boxes. I remember what a job it was to try to find something after we'd moved. I invited her in and led her to the living room. It seemed more polite than sitting in the kitchen again. She told me about the place they'd left in Minnesota—a much bigger house that they didn't need anymore now that their family was grown. They wanted a smaller town and a smaller home. That's why they came to Nettleburg. Friends of theirs who used to live here had told them it was the perfect place to retire, so they checked it out and decided they would come. I hope they like it here.

Tuesday, November 23

Dearest Mandy,

I forgot to tell you yesterday: Peg didn't say one word about that lady at church. That made me relax a little more. Maybe someday soon I'll tell her about you. I guess I'll have to before someone at church blurts out the whole story.

Do you think it would be okay if I went over there? Something about Peg draws me to her; I can't even explain it. She was just here yesterday, so I don't want to get pushy. Isn't it funny that I feel comfortable with someone twice my age? See what you've done to me, Sweetie? You've made me grow quite old inside!

Wednesday, November 24

Dearest Mandy,

Tomorrow is Thanksgiving Day. There is so much for me to be thankful for. I have Daddy and Nana and my younger brother, your Uncle Steve. There's Grandma and Grandpa Jurgens, and Aunt Betina and Uncle Jeff. I have friends, though I haven't stayed in touch since you left. I have a nice, old house and pretty furniture that Daddy and I bought when we were both teaching school.

13

Why, when I have all these wonderful things, does the one thing I don't have hurt so much? Why can't I get over you?

Thursday, November 25,
Thanksgiving Day

Dearest Mandy,

We got up early this morning for the four-hour trip to Grandma and Grandpa's. We really don't see Daddy's folks as often as we should. They live on a farm, and it's hard for them to get away. Daddy works hard all week, and I know he doesn't feel like putting in a trip on the weekends. We did go more when you were here. We knew how much Grandma and Grandpa loved to see you.

It was good to be back on the farm. Grandma is a wonderful cook. I couldn't eat much, but even my appetite is better with Grandma's good food. Amy and Alan are nice people, and Dillon is a typical two-year-old. He really hammed it up with everyone watching him.

Strangely enough, seeing Dillon didn't bring on a wave of pain and tears. Maybe because he's a boy and older than you. Maybe because everyone was having a good time. Whatever it was, I didn't look at Dillon and see you. I saw only a bright, happy child who was bringing all of us joy on Thanksgiving. For me, that's a small victory.

Friday, November 26

Dearest Mandy,

Something strange happened today. I was tired from the trip to the farm, but I slept restlessly last night. I didn't

14

get up until eight o'clock. When I came downstairs, Daddy was standing by the window, looking out. I know he didn't see me. I came down quietly and stood beside him. He started when I touched him, and I saw tears in his eyes before he spun away and left the room.

I wanted to run after him, hold him, comfort him; but something stopped me. He's been irritated with me so often that I wasn't sure it was the right thing to do. Is it possible? Could Daddy still be hurting as much as I am?

Saturday, November 27

Dearest Mandy,

It's lonely here today. Peg and Stan are still gone. They went to spend a few days with their daughter and her family over the Thanksgiving holiday. Daddy's a big grouch. I don't know if he's still upset that I saw him crying yesterday, but he's barely talked to me. Right now he's holed up in his study, correcting papers on the Civil War. He's a good teacher, Mandy; he would have taught you so much. Maybe he would have been your high school teacher someday. I think I'll just leave Daddy alone this morning, or we might have our own "civil war."

Sunday, November 28

Dearest Mandy,

We went to church this morning, but I couldn't keep my mind on the sermon. I saw your little white coffin up there, right by the altar steps. A spray of pink rosebuds lay on top. Before the funeral, I got to see you one last time. You looked like a beautiful doll in your new red dress, the tiny cross your godparents gave you glinting around your

15

neck. Your fingers were curled again, your hair a gentle golden halo around your head.

Sometimes that scene unwinds as I sit in church, springing like an unwanted demon from my soul. I try to push it away, to concentrate on what Pastor's saying, but all I hear are muffled sobs echoing from the pews. I feel my cheeks wet with tears, and the muted scent of roses lingers in the air. I am in another time, another place. Or is that the true reality and the here and now an empty dream? Sometimes I cannot tell.

Monday, November 29

Dearest Mandy,

Nana called today. She spent the holiday with Uncle Steve. He's studying to be a doctor, and it was difficult for him to come home. So Nana, trooper that she is, drove up to see him. In fact, she brought the whole dinner with her. How fortunate I am to have two great cooks in the family! I'm sure Uncle Steve enjoyed it. Eating and pestering me were his favorite pastimes when we were growing up.

Nana wanted to know how I was doing. I lied and told her fine. Otherwise she worries about me. "How are you doing?" I asked.

I could hear the sadness in her voice. "Not too well," she said. "I miss Mandy so much. She was my first grand-child. I don't know why God took her."

We've had this conversation many times before, Nana and I. I wish she lived closer. As it is, we don't get to see each other much. I knew it would be hard when Daddy took the teaching job in Nettleburg, but I didn't know how hard. Nana did come to stay with me for three weeks after you left. We spent a lot of time crying together, remembering you and the joy you brought into our lives.

In some ways it's almost worse for Nana than for me. My dad, your grandpa, died of a heart attack a year before you were born, so Nana's had a double loss. She wasn't over his death when suddenly another bright light in her life was taken away.

When you were born, I felt badly that my dad wasn't alive to see you. I knew how much he'd have loved you. Now I'm a little jealous that he has you all to himself in heaven.

Tuesday, November 30

Dearest Mandy,

Peg called today to ask if we had a good Thanksgiving. Wasn't that nice of her? I told her about Grandma's wonderful meal and the fun we had with Dillon. She said they had a good time too. Her daughter has twin girls who are ten years old and a boy, eight. I can tell how proud Peg is of them.

Peg asked if I'd like to come over and share some pumpkin pie. Her daughter packed up lots of leftovers, more than they can eat. Sounds like Grandma Jurgens. (Although we didn't have any pie left to take home.) I was glad to go over to Peg's and visit.

We sat in the living room on a flower-splashed sofa. Peg and Stan have everything pretty well organized. I don't know if I was that speedy at unpacking. There were family pictures everywhere. The one I liked best was a big one of three girls and a boy, hanging on the wall over the fireplace. The girls were wearing matching frilly pink dresses. And the boy, who had the biggest smile, wore blue plaid pants. I think from the style of the clothes and hair they're Peg's children and not her grandchildren. They were adorable— almost as cute as you!

of my endless days. At n

the house is still, your spirit

Dearest Mandy,

I'm feeling sorry for myself today. Maybe it's because I was at Peg's yesterday. Seeing the pictures of her children and grandchildren made me think of you, and it doesn't seem fair that she has four children and I have none. I know she can't help it, and I know I shouldn't feel like that, but here I am, pouting and teary eyed again.

Maybe I'm feeling this way because it's December. The stores and TV and magazines all shout the joy of Christmas, and I don't feel any joy at all. Last year I did nothing, absolutely nothing. No tree. No cards. No decorations. I have to make myself do it this year, or Daddy will be upset. What will I write in the cards? Everyone knows about you, so I guess I don't have to write much. Just enough to be polite.

I haven't bought any presents at all. I used to be so far ahead with everything. Now I don't even care.

Maybe Peg will go shopping with me. I must tell her about you. I just must. Why is that so hard to do? Another one of my *whys*, Mandy. I have lots of them!

Dearest Mandy,

Mrs. Mueller—you remember her, the lady down the street who always aahed and cooed over you when we went walking—she told me that God needed my baby to be his angel. I don't believe that. Babies don't turn into angels, and God wouldn't have to yank people's babies from earth to make more angels for himself. And, yet, sometimes I wish I could believe that, could believe that you were flying around in heaven somewhere with tiny wings, watching over us. Maybe that would bring me some comfort, at least more than my eternally asking, "Why, why, why?"

Where is God, Mandy? He used to seem close, and now he's far away. I try to read the Bible. I cry to him, but all I find is silence. I want to pray, but I have no words. What do I say to a God who tells me he loves me and then snatches back my baby?

Friday, December 3

Dearest Mandy,

I shouldn't have talked to you about angels yesterday. Last night I dreamt that I went into your room. There was a light coming from your bed, and when I walked over to it, there you lay, smiling and holding out your arms. Your hair was shining and golden, your face almost sparkled, and your smile was radiant. It seemed as though a shimmering light surrounded you, and I knew, oh, I knew that you were happy in heaven. I reached to take you, and like a spirit, you slid through my arms. When I looked down into your crib again, it was dark and empty.

I wonder what it means.

Saturday, December 4

Dearest Mandy,

Daddy was so grumpy this morning—again! He always used to be happy, the one I could lean on. Now everything's changed. I'm afraid to talk to him, although my heart cries for him. The chasm between us has grown into a gorge, and I don't know how to cross it. After breakfast he went into his study and closed the door, which means "KEEP OUT." I did.

20

Dearest Mandy,

Daddy and I went to church alone today—a silent trip. Daddy was asked to be a substitute usher at the late service. Peg and Stan went to the early service since they were meeting friends (the ones who prompted them to move to Nettleburg) for dinner, and the late service does often get quite late.

It was probably a good thing they didn't come with us. There was a baptism. I bit my lip and clenched my hands until they hurt, but the tears still squeezed out. I was seeing you in the long eyelet dress—the same one I wore at my baptism—wrapped in the snowy white blanket Nana knit just for you. Uncle Jeff, Aunt Betina, and Uncle Steve were your sponsors; we got the whole family involved!

I stared at the baptismal banner that the family would take home, but I didn't see the baby's name. Instead, on the smaller, removable banner that hung on the big one, I was reading your name: MANDY SUE JURGENS. Right below the blue felt letters were the beautiful words "Today God spoke my name." If there is any comfort in my loss, it's that you belong to Jesus. We had you baptized, and God brought you into his kingdom. It's strange that, although my faith is unsure and flickering, I am certain you are in Jesus' arms. I like to look at your banner. It still hangs in the little alcove off your nursery.

Monday, December 6

Dearest Mandy,

Today was not a good day. I guess the baptism yesterday bothered me more than I thought. I tried not

21

to think about you. I did the laundry, vacuumed and dusted, looked at recipes, and took out hamburger for a casserole. Nothing helped. In the afternoon I tried to read a book Uncle Steve gave me for my birthday, but I couldn't concentrate.

Finally, I sneaked into your room and opened the bottom drawer of your dresser. There lay your baptismal dress beside the folded white blanket. It was wrapped in tissue with your tiny booties and lacy cap on top. I picked up each bootie, held it, caressed it. I ran my fingers over the cap, remembering how your blond curls peeked out when you wore it. I carefully unwrapped the dress and held it as though you were in it once again. For a moment I was back there, at the baptism, and you were in my arms.

I must have lingered too long because I didn't even hear Daddy come home. I didn't hear him come up the stairs and into the room until he yelled. And I mean yelled! "What's the matter with you, Carrie? You go around in your own dismal, little world, making everyone miserable. You don't even try to get better! She's gone; she's dead. Mandy is never coming back. Get over it, Carrie!"

I was too stunned to reply, and Daddy whirled around and stormed out of the room. I never, ever thought our marriage would be in trouble, but now I'm not so sure. I feel so lost, so alone. Oh, God, help me!

Tuesday, December 7

Dearest Mandy,

I think we've hit bottom, Daddy and I, and I don't know what to do. Supper last evening was a nightmare of silence. Daddy hasn't spoken to me since the confrontation in your room. After Daddy left for school, I turned on the radio. A psychologist was saying that we have options in life. He said when we're facing a difficult situation, we should list the options, with the one we like best first, down to the least acceptable. It was as though he was speaking just to me.

When the program was over, I wrote out my option list.
1. Talk to Peg.
2. Talk to Pastor Reiwald.
3. Try to talk to David.
4. See a counselor.
5. Leave David.

Wednesday, December 8

Dearest Mandy,

I can't tell you how hard it was to write "Leave David" yesterday. What a terrible thought! Marriage is supposed to be forever; we promised each other that. Daddy and I loved each other so much. We loved you so much. We talked about you, held you, shared you. How strange that the thing that brought us closer together is now ripping us apart. I feel like I'm in a spiraling whirlpool, being pulled down farther and farther, sucked into a drowning abyss.

Things are so bad that I'm not sure there is a way out anymore, but I have to try. Daddy certainly isn't going to do it. I looked at my list again, and I feel satisfied with what I wrote. I don't know Pastor Reiwald very well, so I'd rather talk to Peg first. And I'm not sure how I feel about going to a counselor.

It will be hard for me to talk even to Peg, but I'm willing to trust her. I haven't known her long, and I don't know her well, but I feel a pull towards her that I can't explain. If that should fail (oh, it can't, it can't!), I will talk to Pastor. Somewhere in all this I must face Daddy. Once and for all, we have to talk, whether he wants to or not. I can't give up this marriage without a fight.

Thursday, December 9

Dearest Mandy,

Oh, my dear one, I'm so scared! I called Peg this morning and asked if I could come over and talk to her. I can't do it today; she has a luncheon date and a dentist appointment. She said to come tomorrow for lunch. I wish I could have gone over right away. This makes my agony worse, and I'm beginning to have doubts. Maybe talking to Peg isn't the right thing to do. Maybe I should visit Pastor first. What if she has no answers for me? What if she thinks I'm terrible because I can't get over you and our marriage is in trouble? I hate *what-ifs*, and now my life is full of them.

Friday, December 10

Dearest Mandy,

I'm writing this as I sit at the kitchen table, waiting to go to Peg's. I slept even less than usual last night, and I've just puttered through the morning. My nerves are on edge. I can't think how to begin the conversation. I don't know the best way to tell her about you, about how much you meant to me. I'm getting cold feet. Only the thought of losing Daddy pushes me to trust Peg. What will I do if this fails?

Excuse me, my little one; I was gone a few minutes. I got my Bible and looked up Psalm 121 again. I read the whole thing, not that it's very long. Do you know what the last verse says? "The LORD will watch over your coming and going both now and forevermore." Do you think that means he'll go with me to Peg's house too? I hope so. It's 11:45 now, the time Peg said to come for lunch. I still feel so far from God, but I'll try to picture him walking beside me to Peg's house. Maybe that will help.

Saturday, December 11

Dearest Mandy,

Wait until I tell you what happened yesterday! I got to Peg's, and she had lunch all ready. She made barbecued muffin cups with banana bread and salad. My stomach felt so tight that it was hard to eat, but I forced myself. I simply couldn't tell her about you, and I was beginning to think it wasn't going to happen. I can't believe she didn't press me to talk after I told her Thursday I needed to visit with her.

We talked about the weather and Christmas shopping, which she hasn't done yet either. We made plans to do that next week. I helped her clean up the dishes, and she served the coffee and chocolate cake in the living room. I was getting more and more nervous when I looked up at the big portrait of her children. For lack of something better to say, I asked her about her family, where her children lived, what they were doing.

Oops. I have to stop for now. Daddy just came home from the hardware store, and he doesn't know about this journal. He would get so upset. I'll be back tomorrow—must hide this quickly!

Dearest Mandy,

It's afternoon now, and I'm in the bedroom. Daddy thinks I'm taking a nap, so I can write to you. As I started to tell you yesterday, I asked about Peg's children. She told me her two younger daughters live in Minnesota, while Julie, the oldest, lives about three hours away. Peg didn't say anymore, so I asked, "What about your son?"

Peg was silent a moment, and there were tears in her eyes when she answered, "Danny's in heaven with the Lord. He died shortly after that picture was taken."

I looked up at the portrait, at that darling smiling face with the big dimples, and I got tears in my eyes too. "How did it happen?" I asked her.

Oh, Mandy, she told me the whole terrible story. She was driving to her sister's house with Danny in the front seat. She paused at a stop sign and looked both ways before proceeding. From out of nowhere, a car having the right of way careened through the intersection and plowed into the front passenger side of Peg's car. Danny died at the scene.

"Peg, I'm so sorry," I said. "I shouldn't have asked about him. I know it must be hard to talk about." I felt so stupid. I hate it when people ask me difficult questions, and here I did the same thing to Peg. But at least now I know one thing: I can talk to her about you. She'll understand.

Monday, December 13

Dearest Mandy,

I got so overwhelmed thinking about Peg and all we talked about that I couldn't finish writing yesterday. I put away this journal and lay on the bed crying until I fell asleep. I slept for two hours, the best rest I've had in a long time. When I came downstairs, Daddy had supper ready. He put out lunch meat and fruit and some cookies he'd bought. I couldn't believe how nice he was. Maybe he's as afraid as I am at what's happening to our marriage.

Anyway, I must tell you more about my visit with Peg. After she told me about Danny, I said I'd lost a child too.

"That lovely baby whose picture is on your shelf?" she asked.

I nodded.

"She looks so much like you," Peg went on, "the same curly blond hair, the same big blue eyes. She was as beautiful as you are."

I guess I never thought of myself as beautiful, although I did think you were. I was surprised Peg had even noticed your picture. She never said a thing about it.

"I knew something had happened to make you so sad," Peg said, "but I wasn't sure what. Then I saw that picture, and I remembered the pain—the terrible pain of losing Danny—and I put two and two together. I figured when you were ready you would tell me."

Oh, Mandy, we talked and talked. I told her all about the awful night I lost you. I told her how I cried for you in the darkness, how I still had the nursery, how Daddy and I were struggling with our marriage. Peg took my hand and listened without interrupting me even once. When I cried, she gave me a Kleenex and a hug and waited until I could talk again.

The last thing she said to me before I left was "I'll help you, Carrie. I've been there. And God will help you too."

Dearest Mandy,

Today I actually feel a ray of hope for my life, for my marriage. I want to run to Peg, spend the day with her, to talk and talk and talk. I want to let out all the pain I've kept inside for so long. I can't tell you how much it meant that Peg noticed your picture, said you were beautiful. Other people, even relatives who know about you, come into my living room and pretend your smiling face isn't there. I don't want you to be forgotten, my darling of darlings; I want to remember you always. I want other people to know you, to talk about you, to rejoice in your memory.

I want to go to Peg's today, but I won't. We're going Christmas shopping tomorrow, so we can talk more then. I don't want to make a pest of myself. I'm looking forward to shopping, just because I'm doing it with Peg. It seems strange to be actually looking forward to something. It's been a long time since I've felt a sense of eagerness about anything. Today I will address my Christmas cards. It won't take long. I'm just going to enclose a short note to our closest friends and relatives. There won't be much to say because, as Daddy told me, I've spent an entire year in my own dismal, little world.

Dearest Mandy,

This won't be long, as I'm very, very tired tonight. I do have lots to share with you, but it will have to wait until later. I will tell you that the shopping trip went well. I bought Daddy a book on the American West. He likes the Old West, and it might help him in his history classes. I also

got him a green-checked dress shirt. He wears so many
shirts each week, and I noticed some are wearing out. I
thought the green would look good on him. He's got just
a tinge of red in his wavy hair, and I always think green
looks especially nice on him. I'd like to get him more, but
my finances are limited since I'm not teaching anymore.

I got the Grandmas each gift certificates and Grandpa
a sweater. I bought things for Uncle Steve, Uncle Jeff, and
Aunt Betina too.

Peg and I talked over lunch. I'll share that with you
another time. Good night, my little one. I wish I could tuck
you into bed and kiss you good night. I'll ask God to do
that for me.

Thursday, December 16

Dearest Mandy,

I must tell you what Peg and I talked about at lunch
yesterday. I told her how upset Daddy was with me, how
he just wanted me to get over you. She said that everyone
grieves in his own way, and there was no set time "to get
over it." She also said that Daddy was hurting just as much
as I was, but he couldn't show it. "Why?" I wanted to know.

Peg shrugged. "I think men and women grieve
differently," she told me. "Stan grew up in an era when
men didn't cry, didn't admit to strong emotional feelings.
When we lost Danny, I think he literally didn't know
how to grieve. I was the one who had to help him, once
I understood that."

"How did you find that out?" I asked. (I asked a lot
of questions.) Peg told me that she finally went to a
counselor who helped her work through some of those
things. Eventually Stan went with her. I told her I wasn't
sure I wanted to see a counselor. And I can't imagine
Daddy going at all!

"Let's take it a day at a time, Carrie," she said. "We'll see what plans God has for you."

Dearest Mandy,

Christmas is everywhere. There are carols on the radio, Christmas ideas in the magazines, and holiday shows on television. I wish I felt that Christmas spirit. And I wish you'd had just one Christmas with us. I wanted to see your eyes get big when you spied the twinkling lights on the tree. I wanted to buy you pretty new toys and see you explore them with your hands and mouth and feet. I wanted to take your picture, over and over again on your very first Christmas. I wanted to watch Nana as she held you in your new Christmas dress. And I wanted to be a family on my favorite holiday.

Will it ever be right again? Daddy comes home at night and mutters a hello before going to his study. No hug. No kiss. No family. No joy at Christmas.

I feel some confidence when I talk to Peg, but when I'm home, it's like stepping back into a dark castle where the ogres of grief and pain and separation claw at me constantly. I hope Peg is right. I hope there is hope.

Dearest Mandy,

I've been so busy writing about my visits with Peg that I almost forgot to tell you: Nana is coming for Christmas! Finances are always tight for her, and Daddy and I don't have a lot either. But Daddy and I talked to Uncle Steve, and all of us chipped in to buy her a plane ticket. I know she doesn't expect any more from us, but I did get her that gift certificate so she can pick out something she really wants. I'm going to get a few smaller things too so she has some presents to open.

I do miss Nana so much. I wish you'd had time to know her. She's a very kind lady, and she is a great mom. She taught me how to cook and clean, but more important, she taught me responsibility and respect. She and my dad were the best parents ever. It grieves me that Nana saw you so little, had such a short time to be Nana.

When I talk to her on the phone, Nana tells me we have to trust God, to leave it in his hands. But I hear the sadness in her voice, and I wonder if she really is able to do that. My parents went to church every Sunday and made sure Uncle Steve and I got to Sunday school. But we never really talked much about faith at home.

I took being a Christian for granted. I thought if I asked God to protect me, he would. I thought if I asked God to protect you, he would. Only he didn't, and my faith began to unravel. I haven't been able to put it back together. It's like a skein of Nana's yarn when it gets all tangled. She always says, "Now how did that happen?" That's the way I feel about my faith; how did it get so tangled up? I haven't been able to make sense of it all yet, but I think there's more to faith than just going to church on Sunday. I think Nana and I are both missing something.

Sunday, December 19

Dearest Mandy,

Stan and Peg went to church with us this morning, and then the four of us went out for lunch. Guess what we talked about while we ate: the sermon. It was about the meaning of the word *grace*. I always thought grace just meant Jesus'

31

love for us. Pastor Reiwald said it was God's great love for us, which we did not at all deserve. I guess I'd never really thought about that before. I'm glad I paid attention this morning—those shadows of your funeral didn't haunt me, probably because I was really listening to what Pastor said. Stan said that no matter how many good things we do, we can't earn God's love. That's exactly the way Pastor had put it in his sermon. I felt guilty when I heard that—guilty for the times I thought I did pretty nice things for God and guilty for reminding God often that I was a good mother and he had no right to take you away.

There were so many questions I wanted to ask. Does God always love us? If he loves us, why does he do things that hurt us (like taking you)? If I can't do anything to earn God's love and all the good things I do are spotted and spoiled and utterly disgusting in his sight (that's how Peg put it), why does he love me at all?

I kept all those questions inside, of course. Daddy would know why I was asking them, and we're having enough problems without me making more. Besides, although Stan is nice and I can see his faith, I'm not comfortable enough with him yet to discuss those deep-down things that trouble me.

Daddy was quiet too, but I could see he was listening. From the few things he did say, I knew he had some of the same feelings about faith that I did. I suddenly realized that even in our happier times, when I thought we shared everything, we never shared our faith. It reminded me of Nana and my dad.

Monday, December 20

Dearest Mandy,

Oh, Mandy, it's snowing today! I love the snow. It makes everything look clean and white. I wish I had something like snow to pull over the darkness in my heart. I want to feel happy again, full of life. I want to dance with you in my arms, dance to Daddy with his arms open for both of us. I want whiteness, not blackness. I want life and not death.

Dearest Mandy,

I'm sorry I wrote so little yesterday. I liked seeing it snow, but then suddenly, as I wrote to you, I could feel the sadness creeping over me again, sucking out the desire even to talk to you.

Thankfully Peg called. She asked if I'd like to come over and wrap presents with her. "Bring all the fixings and the gifts, and we'll have a gift-wrapping party!" is what she said. She's too kind to tell me, "I know you need to get out, and I know you need to talk," although we both know why she invited me.

I dragged my stuff over, my shoes crunching on the glistening new snow. Even though we only got an inch, it was beautiful. Peg had hot cocoa waiting. She'd lit a cinnamon-scented candle in the dining room, and it filled the house with Christmas.

We hadn't been wrapping long, paper and ribbons and gift tags spread all over Peg's dining room table, when she asked, "How is today, Carrie? Are you handling it today?"

I shook my head and told her, "Not really." Tears welled in my eyes, and I felt myself biting my lower lip in an effort to keep from losing my composure altogether. Then I explained that the holidays were hard for me, especially Christmas. She nodded with understanding.

"When Danny died, I couldn't bear to go through Christmas. He loved that day so much! Every memory of him tearing open gifts, his cheeks flushed with anticipation,

33

his squeals of delight, tore at my heart. If it hadn't been for the girls and Stan, I would have crawled under the covers and stayed there until the holidays were over."

It was so good to talk to someone who understood— someone who didn't look at me like I was taking much too long to rejoin the human race. I wondered how Peg got her laughter back, and how she came to enjoy Christmas again.

Wednesday, December 22

Dearest Mandy,

Daddy's been home for Christmas vacation this week. Today he hauled our artificial tree down from the attic, along with the boxes of lights, ornaments, and other goodies. We decorated together, and it felt good, even though we didn't talk much. I'm sorry, my darling, but I tried not to think about you so Daddy wouldn't be upset by my sadness. It was hard, especially when I hung the little ceramic rocking horse ornament on the tree. I bought that last September, before you died, because I remembered how much I enjoyed my rocking horse. I hoped that one day you'd have a rocking horse too, and the ornament would always remind you of the fun you had as a child. Now it has only sad memories of things that will never be.

Thursday, December 23

Dearest Mandy,

Well, the gifts are wrapped and under the tree, the cards and Uncle Steve's gift are sent out, and what few decorations we have are up. I still don't feel like Christmas, but at least it looks like Christmas. Nana comes tomorrow;

I'll be so happy to see her. We won't celebrate with Grandma and Grandpa Jurgens until after Christmas. Uncle Jeff and Aunt Betina will be there too. Even with the apprehension I feel at seeing Betina pregnant, I do look forward to being with her and Uncle Jeff again. They're both nice people, and it's not their fault that God took you home.

Peg and Stan won't get to see their daughters and their families in Minnesota, but Julie and her clan will come after the holidays, just like we go to Grandma and Grandpa Jurgens. I invited Tomelson's over for Christmas Eve, but they declined. "We'll get together sometime over the holidays," Peg said. "You need to enjoy your mom and husband without neighbors there too."

I told Peg they were more than neighbors, and we'd be glad to have them, but she shook her head. I wanted to tell her that I was afraid to be alone with Nana and Daddy on Christmas Eve, that I might need her strength to get me through. As if reading my thoughts, she said, "Lean on God, Carrie. He's always right beside you. Remember that Christmas is his day. Think about that wonderful Savior God sent us. Remember that God gave up his Son too, and he understands your pain."

I needed to hear that. I had never before thought of Jesus' coming to earth as God losing his own child. Then I remembered it all led to the cross. Could it be that my grief is his grief too?

Friday, December 24

Dearest Mandy,

What a mess it was at the airport! People everywhere! Grandma's flight was delayed, but Daddy and I didn't have to wait too long. I'm glad the weather was good. I could

35

imagine Nana stranded in some big airport. Of course, she would just sit and knit until her flight finally left, since she never goes anywhere without her knitting bag.

We stopped at McDonald's on the way home for a bite to eat. It was already past six, and I hadn't planned anything for supper. It's hard to plan when you're not sure if the plane will be on time, and it's an hour's drive home from the airport. McDonald's was packed too.

When we finally got our food, Nana looked at my small hamburger (without fries) and scolded, "You should have ordered more; you're nothing but skin and bones!"

Nana always scolds very gently, and I smiled at her. Your Daddy was even quite chatty while we ate. He's always liked Nana, and I think he's glad to have someone to distract me over the holidays.

I must stop now. Nana was tired and went to bed early, and Daddy followed not long after. I wanted to tell you about today, and now I'm off to bed too. How I wish you could have been with us at the airport to greet Nana! It would have made our holiday complete.

Saturday, December 25,
Christmas

Dearest Mandy,

It's snowing today, and it looks just like Christmas should look outside. It's a nice, gentle snow that didn't stop us from getting to church. We'd planned to go last night, but by the time we got home it was too late. I missed seeing the children's service. There weren't many people there this morning. Pastor's sermon helped me remember what Peg said—that this is a celebration of Jesus' birthday. I thought about God sending his only Son to earth, knowing all the humiliation and suffering he was going to go through, knowing he was going to die. Does God cry, Mandy? Did he cry when he sent his Son to such a difficult, sinful place as our earth? And if he knows the pain of losing a child, why did he want me to suffer through that too? I ask too many questions, don't I?

Sunday, December 26

Dearest Mandy,

Yesterday was a busy day, and I didn't have much time to visit with you. We had a quiet holiday, but a nice one. Nana was thrilled with her gift certificate; we're going shopping this week. Maybe Peg will come along, if she has time. I'd gotten Nana some gold earrings and a box of her favorite chocolates too, so she'd have something sweet to enjoy at home.

Daddy loved his book on the Old West, and I guess he liked his shirt. He's not too fussy about clothes, so he doesn't get excited about them. But he needed it, so I know it was a good gift. He gave me a beautiful necklace—a thin gold chain holding a heart pendant with little diamonds around it. I gave him a big hug and kiss so he'd know how much I liked it. Was it my imagination, or was there a remoteness in his return hug, his quick kiss? Maybe I'm overreacting. I know I can do that. Anyway, Daddy's gift was wonderful. I hope he didn't spend too much on it.

Nana knit both of us matching sweaters. They're beautiful! They're off-white, with a burgundy design around the top. Nana is so gifted! I never really took to knitting like she did, although she certainly tried to teach me. Daddy and I tried them on, and they fit perfectly. Mine was just a little big—no wonder Nana was worried that I'd lost weight!

As Daddy and I stood there in the living room in our matching sweaters with Nana beaming proudly, I wanted you there too. She would have made you a sweater just like ours, I'm sure. Wouldn't that have been cute? We'd all have been family, inside and outside. Now even the sweaters can't cover the separation Daddy and I both feel. We might match outside, but on the inside we're two different shades of darkness.

Monday, December 27

Dearest Mandy,

Nana and I went shopping by ourselves. Peg was getting ready to have her daughter and family come tomorrow, so she couldn't come along. The certificate we gave Nana was for the entire mall, so she could spend it anywhere. I think we went into every store, until even my legs were getting tired. I don't know how Nana finds the energy. She finally settled on a light pink robe marked down to half price at an after-Christmas sale. Nana didn't even bring a bathrobe along because hers was so shabby.

After she bought the robe, we went into a little restaurant for lunch and coffee. As I nibbled on my croissant stuffed with chicken salad, Nana leaned across the table. "Is everything all right, Carrie?" she asked. "I worry about you. And then, seeing you with Dave . . ." Her voice trailed off.

I've always been honest with Nana, so I had to tell her. "No, Mom," I said, putting my croissant down, "it's not all right." And I told her about Daddy, his silences, his anger, and the widening gorge between us.

There were tears in her eyes when she answered. "It's partly my fault, I know. I've had a hard time dealing with losing Mandy, and I haven't been much help to you. I just put more burdens on you."

Now it was my turn to get teary eyed. "It's not your fault," I replied. "You're struggling just like I am. I think Dave

38

is struggling too, only he doesn't know how to show it." I told her about Peg and her little boy, and how sharing with her helped me. "You've got to meet her, Mom," I said. "You'll like her. She's given me hope that things can be all right for Dave and me again. She wanted me to talk to him before the holidays, but I couldn't do it. I will though; I will."

"Don't wait too long," Nana cautioned. "You and Dave have a beautiful marriage, and I don't want to see it fall apart."

Maybe Nana should have said *had* a beautiful marriage.

Tuesday, December 28

Dearest Mandy,

Today was another quiet day. Nana and I did a little baking. We made Daddy's favorite spritz cookies and a batch of fudge. Nana was shocked that I hadn't done any baking at all before Christmas. She remembered how I liked to try new recipes every year. I didn't tell her that there's a lot I don't do anymore.

I was surprised when the doorbell rang in the middle of the afternoon. Nana was knitting, and I was thumbing through a magazine while we visited. Daddy was in the study, doing I don't know what. When I answered the door, there stood Stan and Peg, their daughter and son-in-law, and their three grandchildren. I asked them in, thankful that Nana and I had baked. "Oh, we don't want to intrude," Peg said. "I just wanted you to meet some of my family."

Daddy came out of his study and insisted that they take off their coats and come into the living room. Peg introduced everyone, and after all the coats were stashed away in the spare bedroom on Nana's bed, we went into the living room. The girls, Katie and Kourtney, sat primly on the edge of the sofa, their hands folded as though they were afraid to move. They were so pretty, with identical brown curls and big dark eyes. Brian stood shyly beside his mom. I wondered if his nice-looking features reminded Peg of the little boy she'd lost.

Daddy brought out a puzzle he always keeps for "emergency children" as he calls pint-sized visitors. Soon the children were seated at the dining room table busily working the puzzle, while we adults visited in the living room.

I liked Julie and Craig. Julie had the same easy, caring manner as her mom, and Craig and Daddy were immediate friends. I watched Nana and Peg talking, and I could tell Nana was drawn to her just as I'd been. It was a good afternoon, Mandy, full of family and friends, cookies and coffee and a quiet pleasantness. It's the closest to happy I've felt in a long, long time.

Wednesday, December 29

Dearest Mandy,

Daddy drove us around town last night to look at Christmas lights. Nana always enjoys that. (So do I.) The twinkling lights in the cold, dark night were beautiful. Daddy checked the paper beforehand, so he knew where all the best decorations were. We didn't say much; just gawked at each breathtaking display.

In the silence of the night, as we passed a yard with shimmering white lights and a nativity display, I could almost hear the angels singing at Christ's birth. I wonder if Mary really understood how special her baby was. How could any mother comprehend that she was the mother of God? I remember that Simeon in the temple told her that a sword would pierce her heart too. Mary had to wait longer than I did to experience that sword, but we both knew the sharpness of its blade. And the feeling *is* like a sword, Mandy, a deep, sharp cutting right into the heart, where the bleeding never stops.

40

Dearest Mandy,

I wish Uncle Steve were here. I haven't seen him since he came for your baptism. It is such hard work to become a doctor. I wanted him to fly here with Nana for Christmas, but he said he had all kinds of tests to study for, and he really couldn't take the time. "Don't worry about me, Carrie," he said. "I'm not a traditionalist like you and Mom. She needs to get away, and I'm fine here. A doctor who's been a real help to me has invited me for Christmas Day. Honestly, I'm looking forward to some free time to really delve into the books."

I hope he was telling me the truth. We called him earlier this evening, and he did sound fine. He liked the sweat pants and shirt I got him. "Now," he said, "I can do my running in style!" We gave him a booklet of Burger King certificates too. I think he liked that just as much. He said we didn't get any present from him because he'll deliver it in person; he didn't say when. Knowing Uncle Steve, he hasn't even bought it yet.

He talked to Nana and Dave, then got me back on the line. He wanted to know how things were, how they *really* were. I couldn't say much with Nana and Daddy there, so I just told him I was coping. "Your voice betrays you," he answered. "Call me some night when Dave's gone, and we'll have a long talk. I pray for you every day."

I miss Uncle Steve. He has a strong faith, a way of walking close to God that I've never been able to equal. He grew up in the same house I did, but somehow found that accepting, unquestioning faith that I'm missing. I will call him and tell him how much I need his prayers.

41

Dearest Mandy,

Today we traveled to Grandma and Grandpa Jurgens.
We took Nana along, and I tucked this journal in my travel
bag under my nightie so I wouldn't miss a day with you.

There were hugs all around when we got there—Nana
says Daddy's clan makes her feel just like family. Aunt Betina
looked quite pregnant, and it was a while before I realized
that no one had even mentioned the coming baby. I knew
it was because of me, and I knew it wasn't fair. I took a deep
breath and asked, "How are you feeling, Betina?" The words
came out easier than I thought they would.

"Just fine now," she said, smiling gratefully. I know this
whole thing has been difficult for her too. I was suddenly
thankful for the extra present I'd bought her—a set of
checked burp cloths with matching bibs. "You'll use those
a lot," I said after she opened the gift. Daddy looked at
me with a strange expression, like he couldn't believe I
was actually talking about a baby without crying. He
didn't know how difficult it was for me to do that.

Daddy may have toasted in the New Year, but I was
in bed before midnight. Suddenly I needed to be alone,
needed to think about the old year and the new year
coming in. I fell asleep praying that in this coming year
I could finally let you rest in the Savior's arms.

Saturday, January 1,
New Year's Day

Dearest Mandy,

It's cold today—five below zero! I'm glad I brought my
fuzzy purple sweatshirt. It's the warmest one I have. Even
at that, I was still cold; but, then, I've felt cold ever since
you left. The chill in my soul seeps right through my body.

We played card games, and the men watched football
in the afternoon while the women helped Grandma Jurgens
with dinner. As usual, she made too much. She had ham
and turkey, potatoes, and lots of other goodies. I'd be worn
to a frazzle, but Grandma positively beamed when everyone
praised her cooking skills.

The men were still at the TV last evening, the two
grandmas were visiting, and that left Aunt Betina and me
together. "Carrie, is it okay if I talk to you about the baby?"
Aunt Betina asked. I like Aunt Betina's caring, her honesty.

I was honest too. "It's still hard for me to talk about
babies," I admitted, "but I am trying. And I'm excited for
you and Jeff. Yes, you can talk to me about the baby."

How we talked! Aunt Betina had all sorts of questions
about caring for a new baby, and I tried to answer what I
could. "You were such a good mother," she told me once,
with tears in her eyes. "I hurt for you so much when Mandy
died. I want to be the kind of mother you were." Impulsively,
she reached over and hugged me. Tears stung my eyes too.
"Thank you, Betina," I answered. "That's the nicest thing
anyone's said to me." After more than a year of doubting,
wondering if I was indeed a terrible mother, if I had
somehow neglected you, hurt you, it was such a comfort
to hear her words of affirmation. God bless Aunt Betina.

43

Sunday, January 2

Dearest Mandy,

It was a long trip home today. As Uncle Jeff and Aunt Betina set off in the opposite direction, I wished they weren't so far away. We talked a lot yesterday. Aunt Betina wanted to know all about you, wanted to know how I got through it all. She listened, really listened, just like Peg. "Do you think we'll ever know why God lets things like this happen?" she asked. I had no answer. Aunt Betina leaned back and folded her arms across her expanse of stomach. She shook her head. "We probably won't know those kind of things until we get to heaven, Carrie. Maybe life is in the journey and not in the answers."

I'm not sure what she meant by that. I'll have to remember to share it with Peg.

Monday, January 3

Dearest Mandy,

Daddy went back to school today. I think he was glad to get back. Sitting around for two weeks drove him crazy. I thought when he gave me the necklace, things might be better, but it doesn't seem so. Maybe he got the necklace at a good sale, and it wasn't supposed to mean anything. We're two strangers living in the same house. Oh, we talk, especially with Nana here, but we never talk about important things. Just: Do you think it will snow? Where are you going? When will you get back? What do you want for supper? You know, things that have no real meaning. It's as though we've made an unseen pact never to mention your name, never to talk about sorrow or loss or pain or grief. We're human robots, Mandy. I don't understand

44

how other people can look at us and not be able to tell. Of course, maybe we're not as convincing as we thought. After all, Nana knew, and I never said one word to her.

Tuesday, January 4

Dearest Mandy,

I called Peg this morning; I knew that her family had left on Sunday. I wanted Nana to spend more time with her, to really get to know her. Peg said she'd be delighted to come over; she was tired of cleaning up after the visit and needed a break.

Nana and Peg and I had a wonderful visit. Peg told Nana she felt badly when she heard you were her only grandchild. "It's been hard," said Nana, glancing at me, "for both of us." Peg listened as Nana talked about the pain of losing you. "I'm as bad as Carrie," she said. "I can't seem to get over it."

"Nettleburg is small," said Peg, "and I've discovered there's not a lot of help for grieving people. The hospital here has no programs, and I couldn't find any counselors with special training in grief counseling. But your city is bigger. See if there's a support group to join. Check at the hospital. Talk to your pastor. Maybe he's had training in grief counseling. Even if he hasn't, I'm sure he'd be able to help you."

"Dealing with your pain doesn't mean forgetting Mandy," Peg continued gently. "She'll always be your granddaughter. She'll always be important to you. It's okay to take all the time you need to grieve. But if you feel you need help, those are the places I would look."

"Thank you," said Nana, looking straight into Peg's eyes. "I know Carrie and I both have to move beyond the hurting, the loss. I am so, so happy Carrie has you for a neighbor."

"Carrie's been good for me too," Peg answered. "I don't

45

think Stan and I picked this place to retire by chance. I think God chose it for us."

Really, Mandy, that's what she said. Peg seems to believe that God is involved in every facet of life. It's hard for me to imagine that the God who took you away sent Peg to help me heal. Maybe I just need more time to understand.

Wednesday, January 5

Dearest Mandy,

I drove Nana to the airport this morning, and I miss her already. The house seems so empty, so quiet. I know this aloneness isn't good for me. That's when I think about you. That's when I feel your presence, listen for your voice, long for the touch of you.

I can't call Peg so soon after our last visit. I feel like I run to her all the time. Maybe I'll go for a walk. It's cold out today, but there isn't much snow left. I think if I bundle up I'll stay warm.

Thursday, January 6

Dearest Mandy,

I did go for a walk yesterday, and it was cold. I remember pushing you in the stroller while the autumn leaves fell over us like confetti. You loved to ride to the park, and I always pretended you listened as I chattered all the way there. I found myself tugged unwillingly down the paths we used to walk, down the sloping hill to the playground on the other side. It was strangely silent there without the children. The swings swung gently in the winter breeze, and I imagined summertime and a little girl with long blond curls begging me to push her. She went higher and higher, her squeals of delight echoing back as I laughed at her exuberance.

Suddenly the picture faded, and I stood there alone, my shoulders hunched against the cold, crying instead of laughing, the tears making warm paths down my icy cheeks. I'll never have that little girl to play with. I'll never hear the laughter or feel her small arms hugging me. Never is a long, long time.

Friday, January 7

Dearest Mandy,

I'm so afraid. The days are slipping by, and I still haven't talked to Daddy. Peg says I'll know when the time is right, but no time seems right to me. Nana called today and, as if reading my thoughts, asked if I'd spoken to Daddy yet. I told her I would this weekend, and now I have to do it. Maybe, scary as it is, that's the best way. Just make myself tell him we have to talk. Then all those what ifs start clawing at my mind, and I wonder what I'll do if Daddy won't discuss anything, won't admit our marriage is falling apart. Peg says not to worry so much, to leave it in God's hands. But I left you in God's hands, and look what happened.

Saturday, January 8

Dearest Mandy,

I made Daddy blueberry pancakes this morning. I took a bite, then put my fork down. "Dave," I said, "we have to talk."

"Oh, is that what this is?" he asked. "You fix me a nice breakfast to humor me so I'll listen to all your complaints?"

I willed myself not to cry. "I do want to talk to you," I

47

said, choosing my words carefully. "I'm worried about us. Ever since we lost Mandy, things haven't been the same. There's no joy in our lives anymore. We never touch or talk about anything important. Dave, . . . I'm worried about our marriage."

Daddy put his fork down and stared at me, a cold, icy stare that I thought he saved only for the worst of misbehaving students. "What's to talk about, Carrie? Every time you want to talk, you end up crying. I'm tired of it. I'm tired of trying to make you feel better, tired of coming home to constant gloom. I can't bring Mandy back, Carrie. What in the world am I supposed to do?"

Daddy threw down his napkin and stormed out of the kitchen. I sat there, staring at the cold pancakes, crying again, wondering where it all went so wrong.

Sunday, January 9

Dearest Mandy,

Daddy and I rode to church today as though nothing was wrong. He didn't say much to me, but at least he was more pleasant than he was yesterday afternoon. What do I do now? Where do I go? Perhaps I should visit with Pastor Reiwald. It's just that I don't know him very well. I do know he's really busy, and I hate to bother him. Will I just be another problem for him, another person who needs his help? I overheard his wife say one Sunday after church that it seems like she hardly gets to see him, what with meetings every night and all. I don't want to be another imposition. Tomorrow I will talk to Peg and see what she says.

48

Dearest Mandy,

I called Peg this morning and asked if she had some time for me today. "Of course!" she said, as though there was nothing more important in her life.

When she came, I told her what happened with Daddy, asked her what I should do now.

Peg was silent a moment, thinking. "Talking to Pastor Reiwald might be a good idea," she said. "Maybe you can talk to him alone, and then bring Dave later."

"If Dave will come," I answered, hating the bitterness in my voice.

Peg reached across the kitchen table and laid her hand over mine. "We'll pray, Carrie," she said. "You can't change hearts, and I can't change hearts, but God can."

Oh, Mandy, her words touched me. "I'm not sure I even know how to pray anymore," I told her. All the pain came rushing over me, and I put my head down on my arms and sobbed.

Peg scraped her chair closer to mine, and I felt her arms around my heaving shoulders. She didn't say a word; just let me cry. I didn't want her to see me like that, but I couldn't stop. Finally, with no tears left, I raised my head. "It's been so hard," I told her haltingly, between gulping sobs. "I feel guilty that Mandy's gone—I was her mom; I should have saved her. Part of me doesn't blame Dave for his anger. Part of me says I deserve it, that I must have done something wrong or she wouldn't have died."

"What does the other part of you say?" Peg asked.

"It says I did the best I could, that I did nothing to hurt her, nothing to make her die. In fact, from all I've read, Mandy didn't fit the characteristics of a SIDS baby. I was nursing her, I put her to sleep on her back, she wasn't premature. All she had was a little cold. Lots of babies get colds and don't die of SIDS." I took the Kleenex Peg offered and blew my nose.

"Have you ever thought why God allowed you to do everything right and still took Mandy?" Peg said. I shook my head. "Maybe it's so you would know it was nothing you did, but something he did."

I started to cry again. "But, why, why would God take my baby? Why would he do that?"

This time Peg shook her head. "I don't have the answer, Carrie," she said. "I wondered, over and over again, the same thing about Danny. I know I looked before I pulled out into the intersection that day. I was always careful. Where did that car come from? How could I not have seen him?"

"Then, one day, I was reading Psalm 139, and it struck me. Seven years was all the time allotted Danny. It had nothing to do with me!"

I wondered what the psalm said. Peg asked for a Bible, and I brought her the almost new one sitting on our bookshelf. She thumbed through it quickly to get to the psalm, then read, "All the days ordained for me were written in your book before one of them came to be."

"Don't you see, Carrie," Peg said, her eyes shining. "God only planned for Danny to live seven years. That was the time allotted him. And he only planned for Mandy to live a few months. I think God took her even when you did everything right so you would understand it was nothing you did; it was his decision before Mandy was even born."

I took the Bible from Peg and read the words for myself. Yes, Mandy, that's exactly what the verse said. I'm afraid we didn't get very far on our "Daddy discussion," but I had acquired a whole new way to think about your going home to Jesus.

Dearest Mandy,

Daddy had a meeting tonight, so I called Uncle Steve. It seemed strange to be looking to my little brother for help; I was always the one who helped him. I told him about my talk with Peg, leaving out the crying part, of course. I got my Bible and read Psalm 139:16 to him and told him how Peg explained it.

"She's right, Sis," he said. "God didn't take Mandy because he was punishing you or because you weren't a good mother. I can't tell you why it happened either, but God knows why. Maybe sometime in the future you'll find some answers, but there's no guarantee."

Then he asked how Daddy was doing. I told him about all our problems, about how we couldn't talk. I said I didn't know how to reach Daddy. I'm sure Uncle Steve heard the strain in my voice.

"Are you praying, Carrie?" he asked. "God can change things."

That's just what Peg had said. I explained how it was hard for me to pray, since God was the one who took you, and no matter how I tried, I still didn't feel at peace with that.

"I think Dave and you both need my prayers," Uncle Steve answered. "Have you talked to your pastor yet? Maybe he can help."

"I've been thinking about it," I told him. "But he's so busy. Maybe my problems aren't big enough to bother him with."

"CARRIE!" Uncle Steve was almost yelling, "That's what he's there for! He's your shepherd, for goodness sake. Has he ever been to see you, to talk to you?"

I told him Pastor Reiwald hadn't come over, but that he had become our pastor after you died. I told Uncle

51

Steve I didn't think he even knew about you and what had happened.

"Well, you call him first thing tomorrow," Uncle Steve said firmly. "And then let me know what happens."

It's so easy for other people to tell me what to do, but it's hard for me to follow through. I hardly know Pastor Reiwald. What will he think of me for my doubting, my tears? Will he understand?

Wednesday, January 12

Dearest Mandy,

I didn't call Pastor today, but I did call Peg. She was so kind. She said she'd call Pastor for me and explain the situation. I guess she could tell I was a bit intimidated about the idea of talking with him. I remember that as a child, I thought the pastor was next to God. Since we weren't particularly active in church, the pastor seemed like a remote being, especially when he stood way up there in that pulpit. In confirmation class my pastor never smiled, and I remember being in awe of him. I worked hard on my lessons every week, more out of fear of him than out of love for God. Pastor Reiwald laughs a lot, and he doesn't seem scary. Nevertheless, just the word *pastor* unlocks my insecurity and a lot of inner trembling.

Thursday, January 13

Dearest Mandy,

Peg called and said she talked to Pastor Reiwald. He wanted me to call him as soon as possible so we could get together. My stomach knotted just thinking about it.

"He's really very nice," Peg said. "We had a good visit. He felt badly not knowing what you were going through. He'd heard about Mandy, but since you never talked to him, he assumed Dave and you were okay. He felt terrible that he hadn't done more to help you."

"I'll call him right away," I told Peg. I knew if I didn't do that immediately, I'd put it off. I felt torn between wanting to talk to him and being absolutely petrified. What is the matter with me, Mandy? Like Steve said, Pastor Reiwald is my shepherd. I shouldn't feel this frightened.

I looked up the church number and called. I was surprised when a woman answered; I had forgotten he had a secretary. "Oh, yes," she said when I told her my name, "Pastor said any afternoon next week would work, except for Thursday. When would you like to come?"

I wanted to tell her I didn't want to come at all, but instead I asked if Monday would work. "I'll put you down for Monday," she answered in a voice like a softly bubbling fountain, and I sensed her genuine kindness. "Would one o'clock be too early?"

I told her that would be fine. Now I have to wait three whole days to get this over with. What will he be like? What will he say about Daddy? I wish you hadn't left, Mandy. See all the scary stuff I have to do because you're gone?

Friday, January 14

Dearest Mandy,

It's snowing really hard today, big flakes that tumble silently to earth, as if in a hurry to blanket everything in peaceful whiteness. At least there's no wind. I wanted to show you the snow, to watch the surprised expression on your face when the wet blobs hit your rosy cheeks.

There are some hills in Nettleburg, and one of them winds between our house and Daddy's school. I hope Daddy gets home safely. I always worry on days like this. Nettleburg's not a big city, but there's still enough traffic, and that hill can be a terror to navigate in bad weather. I'm going to turn on the weather report and see if it's going to get worse. Daddy will be free to leave school in 45 minutes, and it takes him 10 minutes to get home, maybe a bit longer today. He should be here by 4:15.

I'm back Mandy. It's five o'clock now, and no word from Daddy. He has a cell phone for times like this. Why doesn't he call me? It's snowing harder now, and I just heard the ambulance siren. I pray it's not for Daddy.

Saturday, January 15

Dearest Mandy,

Daddy finally made it home, but I was a nervous wreck by the time he got here at 5:30. "Why didn't you call?" I asked, after he told me he was delayed because an accident had blocked the road. I was still shaking from fear of what might have happened to him.

"The cell phone's battery was dead," he answered. "I didn't think you'd worry about me."

"Not worry about you?" I said much too loudly. "I love you, Dave. Why wouldn't I worry about you?"

Daddy looked at me strangely and opened his mouth as though to say something, then stopped. "I needed to hear that," he said quietly and went into his study.

What did Daddy mean? How could he think I didn't love him? If only he had held me when he said that, if only he hadn't left me standing like a lonely orphan in the kitchen when I so much need to know I still belong to him!

I hurried and put the overdone roast on the table and called Daddy. He ate dinner, as silent as before, as though that weird little exchange of sentiments never happened. I should have followed him into the study, wrapped my arms around him, and told him again that I loved him. Why do I always hesitate, always cling to my insecurities and fears instead of breaking out and meeting the challenge head-on? I mean to do everything right, and somehow I do it all wrong.

Sunday, January 16

Dearest Mandy,

After church this morning, when Pastor greeted me, he took my hand in both of his when he said, "Good morning." I saw compassion in his eyes, but he didn't breathe a word about our appointment tomorrow. I will thank him for that. Sometimes I feel sneaky, talking to Peg and now to Pastor without Daddy knowing. I'm not used to keeping things from him. But I'm afraid he'll get angry, and I can't bear his anger anymore.

I thought I knew Daddy, but now I'm not so sure. Would I have discovered this quiet anger, this unwillingness to face difficult things when some other tragedy hit our life? I guess I'll never know.

I do know that I've become more determined that I will do all I can to help our marriage survive. Peg said Daddy can't help the way he behaves anymore than I can help thinking about you and crying. That does make it easier for me. We'll see what Pastor Reiwald has to say tomorrow.

Dearest Mandy,

I can't tell you how scared I was today, going to visit Pastor. I drove around the church three times before I had the courage to park and go in. And then Pastor was busy with someone else, so I had to wait. I twiddled my fingers and flexed my toes inside my shoes, wanting to run back outside. Finally the door opened, and my stomach dropped at the same time. Pastor was smiling and making conversation with a young man I didn't recognize. "Just go in, Carrie," Pastor said. "I'll be right there."

I went into his office and sat down in a blue wing chair across from the dark wood desk. A computer sat to the left of the desk with a Bible verse screen saver on it. "Trust in the Lord with all your heart," it read. That's easier to say than do, I thought. The room had a soft feel to it, a comfortableness that was probably meant to put people at ease. It didn't work for me. I looked at the light beige walls with the muted geometric border wallpaper, I studied the pictures of Pastor's family on the desk, and the picture of his granddaughter next to that.

Pastor came in and sat down, not behind the desk, but in another chair close to mine. "I know this must be difficult for you," he said, after commenting on the weather and making a few light remarks. I wondered how much Peg had told him, and I wondered if he sensed my fear. "I want to know whatever you need to share. Tell me about Mandy," he prodded, leaning forward. His eyes were kind, and I knew he wasn't pretending.

I think I talked too much. I told him everything. I forgot about the time. I hope he had no more appointments because I really rattled on. I went from being afraid to telling Pastor every pain in my heart. I shared my guilt, my depression, the brokenness in my marriage. I even had the audacity to ask him how he would feel if the frame with his granddaughter's picture were suddenly empty.

"I would have a hard time," he answered truthfully, tears springing to his eyes. "I love that child."

Yes, we talked about Daddy too. He said he'd first like to visit with Daddy alone, then the two of us together. I asked him what I should do if Daddy wouldn't come. He said if Daddy wouldn't listen to me, then he would call him. I can just imagine how angry Daddy will be when he finds out I talked to Pastor. I think it would be *better* if I talked to Daddy and explained it all. Not good, mind you, Mandy, but better.

Tuesday, January 18

Dearest Mandy,

I called Peg today to tell her about my visit with Pastor Reiwald. "I told you you'd like him," she said.

I confided that I didn't know how I was going to get Daddy to visit Pastor. "Dave won't even talk to me, " I told her. "I can't hold him down and make him listen. He just gets angry and leaves the room. What do I do about that?"

"The first thing you do, Carrie, is pray about it," she said firmly. "God waits for us to come to him with our cares and concerns."

I wanted to remind Peg that God was the one who caused all my cares and concerns in the first place, but I didn't. "I'll try," I responded. I'm sure she was looking for more than that doubtful answer.

"I'd be glad to come over and pray with you." Peg's voice was quiet, but urgent. "God will answer, Carrie. It might not always be the way we want or expect, but he will answer."

"What if I don't like his answer?" I asked, feeling like a stubborn child.

"You might not," Peg said, "but God knows what he's doing and how he's planned to work not only in your life but in Dave's life too. I'll be over in a few minutes."

And, suddenly, there she was. Peg sat down at the kitchen table with me, took my hands in hers and bowed her head. I never felt uncomfortable with Peg before, but now I did. Could it be, Mandy, that I've completely lost my relationship with God and will never feel right about him again? Is that why it's so hard to pray?

"Dear Lord," Peg prayed, "Carrie and I come to you today with many burdens. Help her to heal, to know you as a God of love and to discover your wonderful plan for her life. We also ask you to touch Dave's heart and help him heal. Restore the close relationship they had and bring them safely back into your arms. We ask these things in the name of Jesus, who loved us so much he gave his life to save us. Amen."

I cried quietly as Peg prayed. All I could say in my heart was "Please, God, please," over and over as Peg spoke to the Lord so confidently. I wonder if *please* is a prayer.

Wednesday, January 19

Dearest Mandy,

No, I didn't talk to Daddy yesterday, and I won't do it today. He's sequestered in his study, correcting stacks of project papers from his American History class. That job puts him in a foul mood in the best of times. I'm smart enough to know I'd better wait. There was nothing good on TV, so I got out the shoebox full of pictures of us as a family. I've never put them into an album. I tried once, but it hurt too much.

I pondered the pictures slowly, relishing each one. I cried a little, but most of all, I just remembered. I really must do something with them. Those photographs are irreplaceable, the only tangible proof I have that you really were here on Planet Earth.

I heard Daddy shuffling his chair in the study and hurried to put the box away under our wedding album on the bookshelf. I was brave to take it out at all with Daddy so near by.

Thursday, January 20

Dearest Mandy,

More snow today! I don't think school will let out early. It's just a quiet, all-day kind of snow that adds up, but not quickly. After lunch I went out and shoveled the walk so Daddy won't have so much to do tonight.

The crisp air felt good, and the shoveling gave me a chance to sort through all the questions in my head. I've tried and tried to think of the best way to talk to Daddy, but my brain comes up with a big goose egg. Peg said God would show me the way, but so far he hasn't done much of anything. If only I knew the right words to say, how to approach him! So far everything I've done was wrong. Maybe there isn't a right way at all, and Daddy and I will live in this limbo until we've drifted so far apart that nothing will bring us together again. Sometimes I wonder if that time has already come.

Friday, January 21

Dearest Mandy,

Daddy had a two-hour late start at school today, so I made him a bacon-and-egg breakfast. I don't usually do breakfast; Daddy gets up too early for me. Daddy told me how good it all tasted, but I think he was a bit suspicious. He needn't have been; I learned my lesson with the blueberry pancakes. Right now the way to Daddy's heart is not through his stomach. I'll have to try a different tactic, although I haven't a clue as to what it will be. Maybe Peg can help me.

After Daddy left, I went into your room. I know I have to put your things away. Leaving them there isn't at all good for me. Today, again, just walking through your doorway brought back all the terrible memories of the awful night you left. Daddy keeps insisting that I let Uncle Jeff and Aunt Betina use some of your things. I checked with Aunt Betina when we were at Grandma's, and she said they already had most of their baby furniture. "Besides," she told me, "you'll need it again someday." I didn't tell her that at the present time that was highly unlikely, with Daddy and I barely speaking.

I think I'll wait and see what Uncle Jeff and Aunt Betina get for baby gifts. Then we can fill in with whatever they need from your things. Maybe I'll tell Daddy that when I have an opportune moment. Then he'll see I really mean to share, and that might be the opening I need. I hope it works.

Saturday, January 22

Dearest Mandy,

Oh, my special one, how can I tell you about today? The phone rang about ten o'clock this morning, and Daddy answered it. I was sitting at the kitchen table, sipping my morning coffee. I heard Daddy say, "Oh, no," and I turned to look at him. He put his hand over the mouthpiece and whispered, "Get the other phone, Carrie." I could tell

60

something terrible had happened. I ran into Daddy's study and picked up the phone. Uncle Jeff was talking.

"I took her in last night," Uncle Jeff was saying. "She was having contractions and felt awful. The contractions have stopped for now, but the doctor isn't making any promises."

"Jeff," I said, "is there anything we can do?"

"No, no, not right now," he answered. "All we can do is pray. If she has the baby, there's a chance it could survive, but it's so early . . ." His voice broke.

"It'll be okay," Daddy said firmly. Daddy doesn't know; he doesn't know if it will be okay or not. Even in the face of losing the baby, Daddy still wants to pretend that it's all just fine.

"Listen," Uncle Jeff was talking again. "I just want you guys to know that even if God lets the worst happen and takes the baby, I'll be strong for Betina. I want to be like you, Dave. I know you've been a help to Carrie, and I want to be there for Betina every step of the way."

There was an awkward silence. Finally I said, "You'll all be in our prayers, Jeff. Let us know if there's anything we can do to help."

"Keep us posted," Daddy said. "Call if anything changes."

"I'll call tomorrow," Uncle Jeff replied, "in the early afternoon, unless . . ." His voice broke again. "Please, please, pray for the baby!"

I hung up and went into the kitchen. Daddy was saying good-bye. He put the phone in its cradle and came to the table. "It can't happen," he almost whispered.

"Yes, it can," I answered. "Jeff is right. All we can do is pray. I wish we weren't so far away so I could be there with Betina."

Daddy was silent. At last he got up, went into his study and closed the door, leaving me to beg and plead alone with God for the baby's life. I thought I didn't know how to pray anymore, but the words came flowing from my heart. I told God I didn't deserve for him to answer me, but for the sake of Uncle Jeff and Aunt Betina to please, please keep that baby safe. "This child is in your hands, Lord," I prayed. "I'm sorry if I've been jealous of Jeff and Betina. I want them to have this baby; I want them to know the joy of parenthood." And then my prayer took a totally unexpected turn. "Thank you, Lord," I said, "for sending Mandy to us. Thank you for letting us have her, even if it was for just a little while. If in your infinite plans she was only given four months to live, I thank you that David and I were allowed to be her parents."

I didn't mean to pray that; it just came boiling out. Peg says the Holy Spirit helps us pray. I think he whispered all those words right into my soul.

Sunday, January 23

Dearest Mandy,

After I prayed yesterday, I called Peg. She said she would not only pray, but she would get the prayer chain started at church. I didn't even know what a prayer chain was. Peg said she called someone, who called the next person on the list, and so on. Imagine! All those people are praying for Aunt Betina's baby.

Something else happened today, Mandy—something so wonderful in the light of all the worry over the baby that I'm almost afraid to speak of it. It's like a fragile snowflake, waiting to melt away and bring back the emptiness of my life with Daddy.

Daddy was unusually quiet on the way to church. After church he asked if I had anything planned for dinner. I told him I had some steaks thawed in the fridge, but they could wait until Monday. "I want to take you out to dinner," he said.

We don't go out to eat often—too expensive—so I was surprised when Daddy said that. He seemed agitated, or nervous. It reminded me of the night he asked me to marry him. He was so wrought up that night that I was sure he was going to tell me he never wanted to see me again. Instead, he gave me an engagement ring. I wondered what it meant this time.

Daddy took me to The Wishing Well—my favorite restaurant. It was crowded, and we had a long wait. Daddy still wasn't talking, and now I was getting really nervous.

At last we were seated at a small table in a corner of the dining area overlooking a veranda. In summer the porch overflows with pots of rainbow blossoms. Now the containers sat empty, filled only with the leftovers of our last snow. Still, the little corner spot had a cozy feel to it. Daddy seemed pleased that we were sequestered away from the other diners.

After we'd ordered, Daddy reached across the table and took my hand. I stared at him, startled. "Carrie, what Jeff said about my being there for you bothered me all night. He was wrong, wasn't he? I haven't been there for you." His eyes searched my face.

"No, Dave," I said quietly, "you haven't." I smiled at him, a sad, wistful smile.

"I'm so sorry," Daddy answered, "I didn't know how to help you; I didn't know what to do. I just wanted to forget. I thought if I pushed Mandy out of my mind, the pain would go away. Instead I got angry and depressed and ended up pushing you away too."

I bit my lip and squeezed his hand tighter. "It's not been easy for either of us," I whispered.

"After Jeff called yesterday, I couldn't hide anymore. You were right, Carrie. I shut myself off because I didn't want to hear you, but you were right. We've got to face this thing . . . together . . . if we're going to heal."

There's so much more I want to tell you tonight, my baby, but it's been a long day, and I'm too drained to write anymore. Uncle Jeff did call this afternoon: no change for Betina. The doctor is guardedly hopeful. She'll have to stay in bed for the rest of the pregnancy. It won't be fun, but a baby is worth any cost.

Monday, January 24

Dearest Mandy,

"I wish I could stay home today," Daddy said as he got ready to leave for school. He looked at me with a look I thought I'd never see on his face again, a look of kindness and love and caring. It was still dark outside, and cold, but here in the kitchen I felt an inner warmth that filled me like summer sunshine.

"I wish you could stay too," I told Daddy. I was glad I'd gotten up today, even though the January wind whistling around the house and shaking the leaky windows tempted me to slide further under the covers and hunker down in bed. I needed to be with Daddy this morning. I needed to relish the newness of him; I needed to savor every moment of this awesome change.

I wanted to call Peg as soon as Daddy left, but it was too early. For the first time since you left, I actually felt rested and alive again. Oh, Little One, the pain is still there, a constant dull ache in my heart, but there's another feeling pushing, pulling at my inner being. For the first time in a long time, I feel hope.

Dearest Mandy,

I called Peg yesterday and told her about the change in Daddy. "See, Carrie," she said, "I told you God would find a way to reach him. You didn't have to do anything at all."

I thought about that a lot today. Here I worried and worried about how I was going to talk to Daddy, and everything fell right into place. Did God really plan it that way? I smiled to myself. I could just imagine Peg praying, "Please, Lord, work in Dave's heart to see Carrie's pain." God would listen to Peg. I'm still not sure he listens to me.

Wednesday, January 26

Dearest Mandy,

I called Nana tonight to tell her that things were working out for Daddy and me. She was so happy. She sounded better too. She said she'd joined a support group at church, and it really helped her. "It's good to know I'm not the only one going through this," she said. I was surprised she hadn't told me that earlier; we talk every week. "I wanted to make sure this was right for me," she explained, "before I went and told everyone what I was doing." Just like Nana, always careful, always concerned.

Tomorrow night I'll call Uncle Steve. Daddy was busy in the study tonight, so it was easy to talk to Nana. Tomorrow night he has a meeting at school, so I can talk freely to Uncle Steve. I know Daddy has no idea of how worried I was about our marriage. Right now I don't want him to know that my whole family was concerned too. Someday I'll share everything with him. I'm beginning to think like Peg; I'm sure God will show me when the time is right. Maybe I'm not quite as certain about that as Peg would be, but I am inching out in faith.

Dearest Mandy,

Uncle Jeff called last night. Aunt Betina is doing fine, even though she's not allowed to do anything. I even got to talk to her. I could hear the relief in her voice now that the crisis is over. "But don't stop praying for me, Carrie," she pleaded. "Things could still go wrong."

It's amazing how everyone asks me to pray for them when I'm not even sure God hears my prayers. I want to trust God, but then I remember how I prayed every day for him to keep you safe. Not one of my prayers did any good, and I still can't help wondering if God really listens.

I had to leave for a little while, but I'm back now, Sweetie. It's about 9:00 P.M., and I just got off the phone after calling Uncle Steve. I wanted to do that before Daddy got home. Uncle Steve has a break in February, and he wants to pick up Nana and come see us. That will be wonderful! He was so glad to hear things were better for Daddy and me. It sounds like his work hasn't let up any. I'm glad he's going to be a doctor, even if it is rough right now. He's such a caring person that he'll be great with all his patients.

Dearest Mandy,

The sun is out today, and all the snow is almost melted. I wish you were here. I would bundle you up and take you for a walk. It would be nice to be outside for a little while. Maybe I'll go for a walk anyway and just visit with God. You can come along too, if you want. You know I always hold you tightly in my heart.

Dearest Mandy,

It was so wonderful to be outside yesterday. I walked block after block and asked God lots of questions. Now I have to wait for answers—if there are any. I talked to you too and told you all about snowmen and icicles and sledding—all the wonderful winter things you'll never get to experience. I reminded myself that heaven is far more beautiful than a snowy day, and you really aren't missing much at all. Are you waiting for me, Mandy? Are you peeking around heaven's door hoping to see my face? Some days the only thing that keeps me going is knowing I will someday be with you again. Peg says God promises that.

Dearest Mandy,

Yesterday after I wrote to you and came downstairs, Daddy asked if I wanted to go for a ride. Just asking me to do anything was such a pleasant surprise that I'd have done whatever he wanted.

Daddy didn't say much on our outing, and it was a while before I realized where we were going. My eyes filled with tears when I saw the sign on the entrance: "Living Hope Cemetery." Daddy told me early on I was never, ever to come here. He said that after I came by myself one day and cried for a week. So often I wanted to visit your grave, to sit there and think about you, but I didn't want Daddy to get angry. If he got angry when I looked at your dress, I wondered what would happen if he discovered I'd sat by your tombstone.

But yesterday he took me there, and we went in together, holding hands. There was no one else in the cemetery and except for the trilling of a lone bird, all was quiet. We walked across the crispy snow, around the graves of other children in this special section. At last, near a willow tree, we came to your grave. I knelt down, ignoring the coldness of the icy grass, and ran my fingers over the engraving on the gray marble: "Mandy Sue Jurgens." It was such a little stone on such a little grave! There was a cement bench nearby, an addition that wasn't there the last time I visited. Daddy sat there while I knelt beside you. When I got up, he was bent over, his head in his hands, sobbing.

"I loved her so much," he said. "I've asked God over and over why he took her. Why? Why?"

I held Daddy and let him cry. I knew the question. I just didn't know the answer.

Monday, January 31

Dearest Mandy,

I called Pastor Reiwald today. Daddy was surprised when I told him I'd been to see him. "I'm so sorry, Carrie," he said. "I never intended to hurt you that much."

I reassured Daddy that I understood why he disappeared into his defensive wall. I too was stuck somewhere in my aching heart and neither one of us seemed to know how to break through the pain. Both of us need to learn how to heal. I told Daddy he'd like Pastor, and he said he would go. I think it's almost a relief to Daddy to know he doesn't have to be strong anymore. He's ready to share his load, just like I needed to share mine.

I called Pastor, and his secretary said Daddy could come Thursday night, if that will work. Daddy has nothing going on this week, so I'm sure it will be fine.

After I called Pastor, I talked to Peg. She asked me to come over, and I gladly accepted. We've been in touch via the telephone, but I do enjoy visiting with her in person. I'll let you know what's going on in her life tomorrow.

Dearest Mandy,

I had a wonderful visit with Peg. She brought out her photo albums and shared her children with me. I could tell it was still difficult for her to talk about Danny. She had one album just for his pictures. What a beautiful child! If I miss you, how heartbreaking for her to lose him when she had him seven years!

I learned from Peg yesterday that the pain never goes away. That thought discouraged me. But Peg also assured me that, even though it isn't gone, it changes. "You remember the good things," she said, "the laughter, the joy of having that child in your life. And, little by little, you begin to see how much God loves you and how your loss was meant to bring you closer to him."

I'm not that far yet, Mandy; but something is changing in my life. I can say your name without breaking into tears. I have more quietness in my soul now, though I still long for you. Peg says it takes time, and time is one thing I certainly have.

Wednesday, February 2

Dearest Mandy,

I called Aunt Betina this morning. We didn't talk long; it gets too expensive to do that in the daytime. But I just had to find out how she's doing. "I'm bored silly," she told me. "I wish you were closer." I wish I lived closer too. We've never had an opportunity to really get to know each other, and I discovered at Thanksgiving how much I like her.

69

"At least the contractions have stopped and the baby's staying put. As much as I hate lying around, I'll do anything to help the baby," Aunt Betina said. She paused, then continued, "Carrie, there's something I need to ask, and I want you to tell me honestly how you feel about it."

My heart thumped, and my hands turned cold. Since you've left, everything unexpected puts me into *flight mode*. I wondered what Aunt Betina wanted to say.

"Jeff and I didn't tell you we're having a girl," Aunt Betina said. "We thought it might be hard for you to know. But the time is getting closer, and we want to honor Mandy. We'd like our baby's middle name to be Mandy, if that's okay with you and Dave. We certainly don't want to offend you, or make your pain worse, so please, please, be honest."

"Oh, Betina, that would mean so much to me!" I exclaimed. "I'll check with Dave, but I'm sure he won't mind."

"We want to call her Jennifer Mandy," Aunt Betina said. "That way, Mandy will never be forgotten. We'll tell Jennifer often that she was named after her cousin who only lived four months."

I think deep down allowing your memory to fade is one of my greatest fears. Maybe that's why it's so hard for me to get on with life again. In my heart I must believe that while I'm sad, people will continue to think of you. If I'm happy, will anyone remember you? Will they know my heart is broken forever because I held you, loved you, lost you?

Jennifer Mandy Jurgens. It's a pretty name, and best of all, you'll be remembered for many years to come.

Thursday, February 3

Dearest Mandy,

When Daddy came home from school, I told him what Aunt Betina said. "If they want Mandy for a middle name, it's fine with me," he stated, and got back to reading the paper.

"But is it really okay with you?" I persisted. "I mean, are you honestly happy with that?" I was sounding like Aunt Betina talking to me.

"Why wouldn't I be?" Daddy asked. "Are you upset about it?"

"No, not at all," I told him, "but you seem so, . . . so unconcerned. I thought you'd be happier."

"Listen, Carrie," he said, and I was afraid for a moment the bitter, angry Daddy was coming back, "it really is fine with me if they want to remember Mandy that way. Just don't forget that their baby is still their baby, and the Mandy we knew is gone."

I wasn't sure I understood what he meant. Did Daddy think I would pour all my love into Aunt Betina's baby to compensate for losing you just because her middle name was Mandy? Maybe the two of us still have a ways to go. It seems like our thoughts zip right past each other, like parallel lines that never meet.

Friday, February 4

Dearest Mandy,

Last night Daddy went to visit with Pastor Reiwald. I had a hard time staying home and waiting. He got back about nine, and I jumped up when he came in. "How was it?" I asked, remembering how good I felt after I talked to Pastor.

"It was okay," Daddy answered.

"Just okay?" I asked.

"He's a nice man," Daddy said, "but I wasn't all that comfortable talking to him. I don't know why."

That disappointed me, and we didn't say much as we got ready for bed. Curled up under the covers, I wondered if things were ever going to be right again, really right. I had so hoped Daddy would share openly with Pastor, but apparently that didn't happen. Sometimes, Mandy, I get angry, just wanting our old life back, wanting all this hurt and misunderstanding and distance to disappear into the dark recesses it came from. Then I wonder if it's always been here, covered up with our untried happiness in each other, our self-absorbed joy in you.

Peg wasn't home today, so I couldn't talk to her. Maybe she knows how to make the misery go away and our happiness return. I will call her on Monday.

Saturday, February 5

Dearest Mandy,

Uncle Steve called this morning. That was nice, since both Daddy and I got to talk to him. He and Nana are coming on the 12th, and they're staying a whole week! He'll be here for Valentine's Day. I asked Uncle Steve if he wanted me to find him a "sweetheart" for that day. He told me he doesn't have time for romance until he's done with medical school and his residency. Some people manage marriage and medical school, but Uncle Steve always was single-minded. And I know it would be hard to be fair to a wife and family while still going to school.

He will make a great daddy someday, Mandy. He thought the world of you and even went shopping all by himself to get you a pretty pink dress and that bright teddy bear. Can't you see that hulk of a man rummaging through racks of baby dresses? He was so proud that you wore that outfit for family pictures. Maybe I'll give that dress to Aunt Betina. It has too many memories.

Dearest Mandy,

We sat with Peg and Stan at church, and I asked Peg if I could talk to her tomorrow. "Come over anytime," she said. I feel like such a bother, but she always seems glad to have me visit.

Peg and Stan invited us to go to dinner with them. Their treat. Daddy said we couldn't let them do that. "Nonsense," Peg stated. "We didn't get you a Christmas present, so this is our treat."

"But we didn't get you a gift either," I said.

Stan looked at Peg and said, "Some people just won't let you do anything nice for them, will they?" That settled it. We laughed and went to dinner with them.

Stan told Daddy about the bookshelves he was building. Daddy does love to put things together, but he doesn't have many tools. "We could use some shelves too," Daddy said. "I'll have to take lessons from you."

"Why don't you come over and build some with me?" Stan asked. "I have all the tools, and we might as well work together. In fact, I bought too much wood, and you're welcome to use whatever you need."

Sometimes I have a hard time seeing God at work in our lives, but I do see his hand in bringing Stan and Peg to be our neighbors. What wonderful people!

Monday, February 7

Dearest Mandy,

I went to see Peg today. Actually, I sloshed over. The snow is melting into puddles, and you know how our back sidewalk dips and cracks, forming little muddy pools. The sun was out, and I felt a touch of spring in the air, though I know I shouldn't get too eager just yet.

I took off my drippy shoes at Peg's back door, and she gave me fuzzy booties to slip on. She had vanilla flavored coffee waiting. It smelled heavenly! She'd made shortbread cookies, so buttery they melted in my mouth. You would have liked them too. It seems strange to think that by now you'd be eating all kinds of wonderful things.

I do feel guilty about needing Peg so often, but I can tell she likes to have me come so she has an excuse to bake. She is one great cook! If I ever get my heart pieced back together again, it'll be fun to share recipes. I used to like puttering around in the kitchen.

I told Peg about Daddy and Pastor and how disappointed I was. She leaned over and touched my arm, "David isn't you, Carrie," she said. "For whatever reason, it's harder for him to share with Pastor than it was for you. Maybe Dave doesn't know him well enough. Maybe there's a barrier not even he is aware of."

"But I thought this was what God wanted! I always seem to come back to why," I told her. "Sometimes I feel like life is one big obstacle course, and I keep running into walls."

Peg laughed. "Sometimes life is," she agreed. "But it's wonderful to know that God has the master plan in his hand."

I couldn't help but smile. "You are so certain of everything," I told her. "I wish I was."

"God is patient," she said. "There's a verse in Ecclesiastes that tells us, 'He has made everything beautiful in its time.' Someday, in God's own time, life will be beautiful for both of you again."

How I want that, Mandy! Not to forget you, not to pretend you never came, but just to rest in God's peace and have my life beautiful again.

Peg continued, "You know, Carrie, I think you missed something in your disappointment. Do you remember the conversation Stan and Dave had on Sunday? Perhaps it isn't Pastor who's going to be David's confidant, but my Stan."

Of course! They talked about building bookshelves together. What a perfect time to visit, a perfect time to help Daddy heal.

"I think Stan and Dave are quite alike," Peg said. "Stan is a wonderful, loving man, but he has a difficult time sharing emotions. He knows how Dave is feeling."

"Could you, maybe, just ask Stan if he'd talk to Dave?" I asked.

Peg laughed again. "Carrie, you have no faith in me. Who do you think asked Stan to bring up the subject of woodworking in the first place?"

Tuesday, February 8

Dearest Mandy,

Just when I thought winter was over, here it is, snowing again, big, fluffy flakes. The ground's already covered. At least it's almost time for school to be out so Daddy shouldn't have trouble getting home. Uncle Steve, fanatic lover of winter that he is, was going to buy you one of those baby sleds to sit in while we pulled you down the snowy streets. I can almost hear your infectious laugh, and see your sparkling eyes, as we whiz you past the houses and down the hills. If only it could have been!

I miss you, Mandy Sue.

Wednesday, February 9

Dearest Mandy,

I worked at cleaning out the little cubbyhole next to your room for Uncle Steve. I had it neat once, but after you left, I just threw things in there when I didn't want to deal with them. It took a long time, especially since I discovered so many memories. I found the basket filled with sympathy cards and reread them and the sadness, the terrible loss, enveloped me all over again. Still, there was part of me that read those cards almost like an outsider. I found myself thinking strange things, like: This person knows my pain; she's lost someone dear to her; I can tell just by the way she writes. Or, this lady doesn't know what to say; her words never quite make it to my heart.

I wondered what you would say if you sat beside me and read the cards too. I think you'd tell me that people all wanted me to feel better, even if they didn't know how to say it. What would I have said to Aunt Betina if she and Uncle Jeff lost their baby? Even going through that myself, I'm still not sure what I'd tell them. I guess the love in a card says someone cares, whether the words are right or not.

We're going to church with Peg and Stan tonight. It's Ash Wednesday. I remember going to Lenten services as a child, but Daddy and I haven't done that since we've been married. We were always too busy. I'm not too busy now. And Daddy said he'd like to go, so we're going. Besides, I don't think Peg and Stan would accept any excuses.

Thursday, February 10

Dearest Mandy,

I liked going to church last night, Mandy. Pastor talked about how Jesus was disgraced for us. I think I've always believed Jesus suffered and died for all people, but I've never quite understood that he died for me personally. Does that make sense to you? When I go to church now, Pastor's words seem to touch me in a way they never did before. I wonder if that's the Holy Spirit working in me. God must be love if he wants me back after all the terrible things I said about him.

I didn't do much today. I need to finish cleaning out that room for Uncle Steve, but I just wasn't in the mood. I'll have to get busy tomorrow though; there isn't much time left.

Friday, February 11

Dearest Mandy,

I finished cleaning out that little room today. I washed the bedding, swept the floor, shook out the throw rugs, and dusted. That room is just big enough for one. Even the single bed looks crowded in there. We almost used that room for you, but it was so small. These old Victorian houses look large, but the chopped-up space makes some areas hard to use. If we had money, we could knock out walls and turn small rooms into bigger ones. Maybe then your nursery would no longer call to me whenever I walk past it.

I wouldn't do a thing with the little alcove in there, though, or the creaky pine rocker we got at a garage sale. It's a cozy, welcoming place in the midst of a room that haunts me. All the memories in that little nook are happy.

Nana called last night. She's so excited about her trip. Uncle Steve drove to her place today and will stay overnight. Tomorrow they'll fly out. I feel like I should be doing more to get ready. Nana loves to cook, so I hate to have meals all planned and leave her with nothing to do. Daddy and I loaded the cupboards and freezer, and Nana and I will work out meals as the week goes on. I know Nana will be happy to have family to cook for again.

I'm eager to see Uncle Steve too. It will be hard, in a way. The last time we saw him was at your baptism. The house will seem empty to him without you here. He held you and held you as though he'd never get another chance. The sad thing is, he never did.

Saturday, February 12

Dearest Mandy,

It's been a long day. Nana's settled in the guest room, and Uncle Steve found room in the upstairs hall closet for most of his things. Goodness knows they'd never fit in that small room he's in. It felt so good to hug Nana and Uncle Steve again. Uncle Steve looked a little thin to me. Nana noticed it too. I know she'll spend the next week trying to fatten him up. She wasn't too pleased that I was still "way too skinny" either. I told her someday I'd feel like eating again, and she just shook her head. We ordered pizza for supper so Nana wouldn't have to start her calorie marathon right away.

Daddy was glad to see both our visitors too. He's always been interested in medicine and almost became a doctor himself. It wasn't long after supper when both Steve and he disappeared into Daddy's study. I think they're making plans for Uncle Steve to visit Daddy's school next week. All those teenage girls will be entranced by my handsome little brother.

Sunday, February 13

Dearest Mandy,

I introduced Uncle Steve to Peg and Stan after church. Peg whispered to me while the men were talking, "He sure is cute!" I didn't think Peg would notice things like that at her age.

Nana put a chicken in the slow cooker early this morning, so dinner didn't take long to get ready. Uncle Steve asked if he could say grace. "Dear Lord," he said, "Thank you for bringing us all together again. Today make this home a house of healing and not of pain, a dwelling of peace and not dissension. Give us eyes of faith that see your love even in the tragedies we endure. Help us remember that you make all things beautiful in your time. Bless this food to the strengthening of our bodies, even as through the Word and Sacrament you strengthen our faith. Amen."

I think that's pretty much what Uncle Steve said. I was surprised. Uncle Steve hadn't said anything about you since he came. And that "all things beautiful" part—it's almost like Uncle Steve and Peg had talked together, but I know they didn't. Maybe God wants me to remember that verse.

Monday, February 14

Dearest Mandy,

Nana and I spent the morning baking a chocolate cake and decorating it for Valentine's Day. We're going to surprise Daddy and Uncle Steve. Uncle Steve went downtown to browse in a bookstore. Even on vacation it seems he can't leave books alone.

The strangest thing happened as we finished the cake. Actually, Nana was doing all the work. We'd bought those little decorator tubes of frosting so Nana could write on the cake. She carefully spelled out "Happy Valentine's Day," but the words seemed to change right before my eyes. I saw the bright pink frosting oozing into "Happy Birthday

Mandy," and I suddenly realized you'd never had even one birthday cake. I started to cry, just like that. Nana stopped, put down the tube and came and held me. She began crying too, and we had a good old sob-fest together. I felt better then, but it reminded me of how fragile my healing still is. I hope Daddy doesn't ask why the "tine" in "Valentine's" doesn't look quite connected to the other letters. Then I'd have to explain why Nana quit right there.

Tuesday, February 15

Dearest Mandy,

Daddy and Uncle Steve enjoyed their Valentine dessert. Poor Daddy! I bake so seldom now, and I know he misses it. And Uncle Steve ate two big pieces! He said he had to get all the good food he could while he was here. After dinner, Uncle Steve made us all go into the living room and sit down. Then he said, "Okay, everyone, let's talk. How are we all doing in the healing department?" Just like Uncle Steve! He never tiptoes around an issue.

No one said anything at first, so Uncle Steve looked at me. "You're first up, Carrie," he stated. "What's changed— for better or for worse—in the last few months?"

I felt reluctant to share my inner feelings with everyone, even if they are my favorite people, but I knew Uncle Steve wouldn't let me off the hook. So I told them about Peg's help, about visiting with Pastor, about things getting better with Daddy. I realized as I talked that I had more good things to talk about than bad. And, yes, I did finally tell them about the Valentine's cake.

Uncle Steve laughed. "So that's why the last letters looked like Mom wrote them in kindergarten!"

Everyone was getting better, even Daddy, although he didn't say much. It is so hard for him to share. I do see signs of healing in him, though. He smiles more. And sometimes he even hugs me for no reason at all, just like he used to.

But the most surprising change of all came from Uncle Steve. "I've decided to go into pediatrics," he said. "You know what a hard time I've had choosing my field. After Mandy died, I knew God was leading me where he wanted me to go. If I can save one baby, if I can find out why SIDS happens, Mandy's short life will be the reason."

I got teary-eyed and hugged Uncle Steve. Nana said quietly, "Just what we've been talking about in group: good comes out of every situation."

Wednesday, February 16

Dearest Mandy,

Uncle Steve went to school with Daddy today. I think he's going to tell the kids all about the medical field. He'll probably make a few recruits before he's done. I hate to think of Nana and Uncle Steve leaving. I helped Nana bake her "secret recipe" chocolate chip cookies this morning. She wanted to send some home with Uncle Steve and leave some for Daddy. I think the men will miss Nana as much as I will, but not for the same reason. I'll bet Uncle Steve has his treats gone before he gets on the airplane. I know him and Nana's chocolate chip cookies too well.

Nana and I talked this morning, and I even hauled out the box with your pictures in it. We didn't cry, Mandy; we just reminisced about the good times. Nana said I really should do something with those pictures, and I think now I'm almost ready. Nana said she took her pictures to her group meeting, and the people all agreed you were a beautiful baby. I can tell Nana's healing, and the group has been good for her. It's a place for her to bare her soul. It's the way I feel when I talk to Peg.

Speaking of Peg, I invited her over this afternoon so the three of us could visit. I know Nana likes her. Peg came over, and we talked about your photos. Peg said she's done some scrapbooking and thought that might be a way to save your pictures. She said she'd help me get started. I can't wait to pretty up all your pictures for posterity.

Thursday, February 17

Dearest Mandy,

It was wonderful going to church last night with Nana and Uncle Steve. Peg and Stan sat with us too, and we all went out for coffee afterward. Uncle Steve and the Tomelsons carried most of the conversation. They discussed the sermon—all the prophecies pointing to Christ as the Messiah. Nana, Daddy, and I mostly listened. I glanced at Daddy once, and I could tell he was hanging on every word. How do I explain the change that's happening to both of us? We went to church before you left, but more out of duty than out of love. Now we want to go. Church hasn't changed, so it must be us.

I did want to tell you too that Daddy and I are going out to a fancy restaurant tonight. It's Doveland Inn in Bursten, just down the highway from Nettleburg. Uncle Steve gave us that as a belated Christmas present. I'd forgotten that he said he would give us something when he visited. That day I thought he was downtown at the bookstore? Well, he was really checking out restaurants. What a brother! I know he helped Nana pay for her plane ticket too. I appreciate his caring. But I hate to see him spend his hard-earned money on all of us. Trying to go to school and work part-time is tough for him. When I protest, he just tells me there isn't anyone he'd rather spend his money on than his family. How do you argue with that?

Dearest Mandy,

Daddy and I had a fabulous time last night. We left Nana and Uncle Steve playing rummy in the dining room and climbed into our little Malibu, which Daddy even ran through the car wash for the occasion.

Uncle Steve was more than generous with his gift, and inwardly I reprimanded him for giving us so much. Then I remembered his smile and knew his gift was from the heart.

Uncle Steve had given us enough so we could even have an appetizer and wine. I ordered shrimp, and Daddy had steak. Daddy ate most of the appetizer, and I still had to take some of my dinner home. I just don't have the appetite I used to. The food was as wonderful as we had heard it was. But, Mandy, the best part of the evening was just sharing it with Daddy. We talked and talked. We did talk about you, but most of all we talked about us. I felt like the knots in the skein of our life opened a little more, and the bad things began to be rewound into good.

On the way home, Daddy said that we should do this more often. I'm going to find a way to put money away so we *can* do more together. Maybe I can get a part-time job. I'm not sure I can handle it just yet, but perhaps I need to try.

Saturday, February 19

Dearest Mandy,

We took Nana and Uncle Steve to the airport this morning and just got back. The phone was ringing when we walked in the door. Stan wanted Daddy to come over and look at his bookshelves. It must be nice to have such a large, heated workshop.

I feel at loose ends. The house is empty again, perfectly silent. The emptiness in the house reminds me of the emptiness inside me. I feel like I'm doing better, but today my heart aches to hold you again, to snuggle with you, to touch the babyness of you. I know sending Nana and Uncle Steve home stoked up the embers of feelings over losing you. For the first time in a long time, I felt your presence here again, and I creaked and rocked in Nana's old chair, pretending that my arms were full of you again.

Sunday, February 20

Dearest Mandy,

Daddy actually came home smiling yesterday from his workshop visit with Stan. He had a book of easy projects that Stan had given him to look at, and he couldn't wait to share it with me. Daddy's going to buy some wood for bookshelves—he didn't feel right using Stan's. There was a cute little rocking horse in the project book that I liked. "Why don't you make it for Jeff and Betina?" I asked. "Their baby won't be ready for it for quite a while, so you'll have lots of time to work on it when the shelves are done."

Daddy was doubtful about his expertise in making the horse. I know Stan will help him, and it would be a unique gift. It's small, so it shouldn't take too much wood. (Daddy said good wood is expensive.)

"Okay," Daddy said with more enthusiasm than I've seen in a long time. "I'll try it. If it turns out well, I can make one for us too. We might need it someday." He kissed me, Mandy, and held me close. I don't even dare think of another baby, but it felt good to hear Daddy say that. Maybe I'll send him to Stan's every weekend.

Dearest Mandy,

It's a dull, overcast day here today. The snow is melting, and everything is slushy and dirty. I hate days like this. I felt myself sliding into the "dreary day blues" and decided to do something about it. Usually I just slide until I hit bottom, and then it takes forever to pull myself out.

I called my hairdresser. (I smiled as I just wrote that, because I really only go in to get my hair trimmed, so it sounds a bit ostentatious to say my *hairdresser*.) Patsy actually had an opening this afternoon. I told her I wanted a new hairstyle and some highlights. I've never put color in my hair; I can't believe I'm doing that! Nana gave me money before she left. She said I should *have a fling* with it. It did no good to argue that Nana needed the money more than I do.

"Nonsense," she said, "I want you to have it." I think she'd consider highlights and a new hairstyle *a fling*.

Dearest Mandy,

Oh, Sweetie, you should see your mommy with her new hairdo. Patsy shortened my hair and added lovely golden hints to it. Daddy was wowed when he came home last night. "What brought this on?" he asked.

"The day was so dreary that I needed something to raise my spirits," I told him.

"Just don't go too far when you feel down," he cautioned. "I'll get a bit nervous if I come home to find you in fancy heels and a black mini-dress!"

It felt good to laugh with Daddy again, and I was pleased that I fought my way back yesterday from that threatening depression. Of course, I can't run out and get my hair done every time I feel depressed (or buy heels and a mini-dress), but I learned that I can change the direction my mood is going instead of just letting bad feelings happen. Maybe I latched on to one small piece of the *getting better puzzle*.

Wednesday, February 23

Dearest Mandy,

I called Nana last night and told her how I'd spent her gift. She laughed and said I should send a picture. I called Betina too. She's doing well and is getting quite eager for that baby. Her due date is in just a month. I know she's happy to have made it this far and feels good that if the baby does come early, at least she'll have a good chance at survival now.

You know, Mandy, I never realized the path to motherhood was strewn with so many frightening obstacles. I thought you got married, had babies, and that was that. You taught me never to take life for granted. I guess when I think of all the people I love, it's a good thing to remember. It took the tragedy of losing you to realize how uncertain life is. Peg says we're like dust and grass: quickly here and gone, quickly blown away. You were a quiet, warm breeze that passed gently through our lives. I'm glad you touched us.

Thursday, February 24

Dearest Mandy,

This morning I was rereading the sermon text from last night—you know, those words in Isaiah 53:5: "But he was pierced for our transgressions, he was crushed for our

86

iniquities; the punishment that brought us peace was upon him, and by his wounds we are healed." I jumped when the phone rang. It was Peg, asking if I was ready to scrapbook. I said I certainly was, but first I had to ask her about Pastor's sermon. "What does it mean that Jesus brought us peace?" I asked her. "I haven't felt that peace."

"The peace Jesus won for us is always there for you," she answered. "I know that peace is difficult right now for you to feel, but it's there. I see you and Dave searching, and Jesus promises in Matthew that if we look, we'll find, if we knock, he'll open the door. Keep looking, Carrie, keep knocking and searching. It's there."

I thought about her words when we went downtown to buy supplies. I know I have a lot more searching and knocking to do.

But the searching and knocking faded from my mind when we picked out scrapbook supplies. There were so many things to choose from, Mandy, and it all cost so much. Peg steered me to the basic things and helped me pick out a kit of baby papers and stickers. She said not to worry— she had plenty of paper and supplies if I needed anything else. I wondered what I'd gotten myself into. I never realized I needed so many things just to decorate your pages. I bought a scrapbook too, and hoped Daddy wouldn't think I'd spent too much on everything. He's usually pretty understanding because he knows I watch our pennies.

Oh, Mandy, it was a wonderful afternoon! I only got two pages done, since putting a page together takes a lot longer than I figured. I started with a picture of your final ultrasound. I remember studying that picture over and over, checking your nose, your head, your tiny hand uplifted as though you were waving at me.

On the next page, I put several pictures Daddy took while I was pregnant with you. I look ecstatic, excited, totally in love with you, the beautiful baby I'd only glimpsed in grainy black and white. I want the world never to forget how much I loved you even before you were born.

Friday, February 25

Dearest Mandy,

I showed Daddy my new scrapbook yesterday, and he seemed impressed. "That's just great," he said. "See? I knew there was a hidden artist in you. I always thought your bulletin boards at school were really well done too." I'd forgotten all about those humungous bulletin boards. Actually, those teaching days of mine seem like they belong to another era, another place. I enjoyed teaching, but I honestly don't miss it at all. Daddy's words made me happy.

I will do the very best I can on your scrapbook, Mandy. I didn't even cry while I worked on the pages, my little one. Peg and I laughed about all the problems of pregnancy and shared some not-so-pleasant memories. I was shocked when I came home and discovered I hadn't shed one tear. I think from what Peg said ("This was fun, Carrie!") that she noticed it too.

Saturday, February 26

Dearest Mandy,

It's a warm, sunshiny day today, and I remembered walking to the park on just such a day as this when I was expecting you. It was February then too, and so warm that I met several moms walking their little ones. I looked at each baby and wondered what you would look like. I imagined pushing you in your stroller, prouder than any of them, glowing in the knowledge that I was a mother too.

We walked often, Mandy, after you were born. Sometimes it was in the early morning as the blistering summer sun made midday quite unpleasant. But, always, I found time for just the two of us. I'm glad I did.

Dearest Mandy,

Daddy's over at Stan's this afternoon, working on bookshelves and checking on that rocking horse. I hope Stan thinks Daddy knows enough about carpentry to make it.

We started cleaning out your room yesterday. It was hard, but I know Daddy's right. I must get on with life, and the first step is taking your short life (but not your precious memory) out of that place that's become for me both a refuge and a hell.

For now I'm putting things into the little room that Uncle Steve used and moving the single bed that's in there into your room. Daddy helped me take down your bed, and I tried not to remember those golden curls against your cold, pale forehead the night you died. Daddy told me he would always remember the little smile you sometimes had as you slept. "I wonder if she was dreaming about heaven," I answered.

Daddy got tears in his eyes. "I know she's there, Carrie," he answered. "Stan reminded me of the Bible story of King David and the death of his little boy. When David learned he was dead, he said, 'I will go to him, but he will not return to me.' Someday we'll see her again."

I know you're there waiting for us, Sweet Baby, but, oh, I do miss you. I missed you as we took down the changing table and zipped the baby powder and Q-tips and all the other things you needed into a large plastic bag. I missed you as I folded Nana's quilt and put Uncle Steve's pink teddy bear into a box with your other toys. I missed you as I unplugged the Noah's Ark lamp and took down the picture of Jesus with the children. I missed you every moment I worked in your room. Only Daddy's being there kept me from dissolving completely.

And Daddy? He worked with me quietly, but I knew from his comment about David's son that he was remembering too. It was good to work together, to share the memories and the sadness. When we finished, and the room was empty, I buried my face in Daddy's chest and wept. He stroked my hair and told me he loved me, . . . and that someday it would be right again. Finding Daddy's love once more was the good thing that came out of all this sorrow. Finding you in heaven will make it perfect.

Monday, February 28

Dearest Mandy,

Peg called this morning. She asked if I would like to go to a women's Bible study on the book of Job with her. It will be held Thursday mornings at church, starting after Easter, with one of the ladies in the congregation leading it. Peg says she's heard that Pat Spelling is a super teacher. "I suppose you want me to see that someone else's life is worse than mine!" I teased.

"Not really," she answered, "but you might like to hear what God says about the unanswered questions in our lives."

I'm going to go, Mandy. I really do want to know why I don't have any answers. Everyone there will probably know way more about the Bible than I do, and I'll feel stupid. I've begun to read the Bible on my own, but I'm not quite sure where to start or how to do it. I'll ask Peg the best way to study.

90

Dearest Mandy,

I forgot to tell you: Stan thought Daddy could make the rocking horse, so we're going to the lumberyard after school tonight to buy wood. I know Daddy's eager to get started. I wish we had enough money to build him a heated workshop too, but I'm thankful Stan is kind enough to share his working space. These people are so nice, Mandy. Sometimes it brings tears to my eyes to think God brought them to be our neighbors. Two such perfect people being here for us has to be more than coincidence. And if God planned it, he must love us. It still doesn't all fit together, but I can ponder God now without so much bitterness. I think I am almost ready to live again.

I keep thinking about that Bible class I'm going to with Peg. I know *of* Job, but I don't really know much *about* Job. Peg says she read that book of the Bible over and over when they lost Danny. If it helped Peg, I'm sure it will help me.

Wednesday, March 2

Dearest Mandy,

This won't be too long, my baby. Peg and I scrapbooked all day at her house. Then I had to hurry home and get dinner ready before church. The sermon tonight was entitled "What Is Truth?" Pastor told us that Jesus is the Way, the Truth, and the Life. I remember that passage from John, but I don't think I ever understood it. I thought I understood it, but after you left, I felt as though nothing about God made sense anymore.

Truth for me became your lifeless body, the answer to my prayers ripped from my arms. Truth was a cruel, vengeful God who emptied my life and almost destroyed my marriage. I'm beginning to see things differently now, but, oh, I still have so many questions. And too often I find myself saying with Pilate, "What is truth?"

Thursday, March 3

Dearest Mandy,

Br-r-r-r. It's cold today, and a few snowflakes are twirling through the air. Just when I thought winter might be over!

Daddy and I went to buy supplies for the rocking horse last night. I'm glad that horse isn't too big because the wood was certainly expensive. Oh well, Aunt Betina, Uncle Jeff, and Jennifer are worth it. It seems strange to give their baby a name when she's not even here yet. But it won't be long now. We're giving them your Diaper Genie, the changing table, and the beautiful stroller the teachers at school gave me as a shower gift. They already have everything else. I'm eager to see how they've decorated the baby's room. The wonderful thing is that I can say that now without a twinge of jealousy. Somehow, when Daddy started getting better, it helped me get better too.

That reminds me, Daddy and I never did go back to Pastor Reiwald. I called Pastor and told him that things were improving for Daddy and me, but we'd be in touch if we needed him. I think Peg was right when she said that Stan might be a better match for Daddy. Things never fit together quite like one thinks they will, do they, my sweet?

Dearest Mandy,

We called Grandma and Grandpa Jurgens tonight. They're getting awfully excited about their new grandchild, but I think they're a little frightened too, after what happened to you. "I'd be ready to go myself if we lost another little one," Grandpa said, and I could just imagine his blue eyes tearing up under those bushy eyebrows.

"Don't worry," I told him, "God is in control, and I've been praying every day for that baby. I know in my heart everything will be fine."

Imagine that, me comforting someone else! And what I said was true. I have been praying every day for Aunt Betina's baby, and I have felt at peace about it. Peg just smiles when I tell her that. "You're learning to lean on God," she says. "That's the most important lesson God can teach us—to have faith and trust."

Dearest Mandy,

Here I am again, a Saturday widow. I really don't mind. In fact, if Stan is as good for Daddy as Peg is for me, I'll gladly give up Saturdays with my husband. Daddy comes home happy, sparkling with life again. His joy rubs off on me too, so I hope Stan keeps encouraging him in his woodworking endeavors.

Daddy's pretty secretive about the rocking horse. I think he wants to surprise me. He did finish the bookshelves and put the primer on. I told him I'd paint them for him, and he didn't object. I think Daddy likes the building but not all the putsy things that have to be done afterward. I like the careful, finishing work. Daddy and I make a good team.

I've been thinking of Aunt Betina all day today. Uncle Jeff called last night and said she was having some contractions. They went to the hospital, but the doctor said everything was fine and the baby wasn't ready to come yet. I know it's better the longer she can carry Jennifer, but I'm sure she's getting tired of being pregnant, especially since she's had to be off her feet for so long. She told me that the good thing about that was that she finally finished all the magazines stacked up in her bedroom. I know there will be times after the baby comes that she'll wish she could just lie around. You certainly kept me hopping, but you know I loved every minute of it.

Sunday, March 6

Dearest Mandy,

It's raining today—a drippy, depressing drizzle. Daddy's over at Stan's working on the rocking horse. I'm not quite sure what I want to do, but I know I have to do something so I won't start thinking about you. See, Mandy? I'm learning to help myself. (Although it doesn't always work. Last week one day I started getting gloomy, so I took time out and read a magazine. Unfortunately, I opened to an article about a couple who had lost their baby. Oops!)

Maybe I'll bake. I did find a recipe for chocolate cake squares in that same magazine. Yes, I read the article, and, yes, I cried, but I got over it. I wouldn't have been able to do that six months ago. I guess it's all right to cry once in awhile if you don't let it take over your life. Sometimes I think even when I'm in my old age, I'll still need to cry over you.

94

Dearest Mandy,

Daddy loved the chocolate cake squares. It was an easy recipe, and I actually enjoyed baking again. Every little emotional success like that gives me hope that someday joy will once more be a permanent part of my life. I don't think, though, that the joy will be the same as it was before. Too much has happened; too much sadness has settled into every inch of my being for me to laugh again without an inward tinge of melancholy.

Tuesday, March 8

Dearest Mandy,

I looked at want ads in the paper, but nothing caught my eye. Maybe I should begin substitute teaching. I know I could do that, but I'm not sure I want to. I can't imagine why I feel this way. I'm not even sure it has anything to do with you, my baby. I did love teaching. But I hated spending almost as much time disciplining as teaching. All the paperwork wasn't much fun either. Daddy never seems to get done. I remember when I taught, we would eat a quick supper and spend the whole evening correcting papers or doing lesson plans. At ten o'clock we went to bed. Not what you'd call a terribly exciting life. I can't even imagine teaching and raising a child. Maybe some people can do it, but I'd be worn to a frazzle, trying to do justice to everything.

And yet, I have this persistent little nagging inside that keeps telling me that I want to do something. The nagging hasn't been there long—only since I've begun to feel better. I know it's a good sign that I want to do anything at all. I think I'll follow Peg's advice and "wait on the Lord." After all, I worried so much about confronting Daddy when everything was wrong in our life, and Uncle Jeff's phone call resolved it, without me doing anything at all.

Wednesday, March 9

Dearest Mandy,

I did scrapbooking with Peg again today. She shared some stickers of a white Bible and crosses, and I used them to decorate the page with your baptism pictures. Actually, I had to do two pages of pictures, since we took so many of you that day. I didn't make it through this afternoon as well as I did last time. My favorite picture is of Daddy holding you, beaming with pride as he looks at you sleeping peacefully, a breathtaking beauty in your long white dress. I couldn't stop the flood of tears.

"We loved her so much, Peg," I said. "I try not ask why, but sometimes the question just comes. I read about people abusing their children or aborting them, and I think how much we loved Mandy, how hard we worked, even when she was a baby, to be good parents, and I can't understand why God took her."

"Carrie," Peg answered, "I don't know why. I can only tell you that for me, God worked miracles in my heart that wouldn't have come if I hadn't lost Danny. And I doubt that he would have put me in your life if I hadn't suffered that terrible loss. How could I help you if I didn't really understand from my own personal experience? Part of why God allows difficult things to happen is so that we can help others. God is part of every moment of our lives, and nothing happens by chance."

Nothing happens by chance. I see that more clearly now than when you were here, but I still wish God would give me answers. Maybe I could accept losing you if God sat down next to me, held my hand, and explained why.

You're smiling at me, you little imp! I can see your big eyes looking down at me from heaven, all lit up with joy. You understand why, don't you? Someday maybe I will too.

Thursday, March 10

Dearest Mandy,

I don't have much time to write because I promised Daddy I'd paint those bookshelves today. He really does need more in his study. But before I get busy with that, I'm going to read my Bible. Peg said I should try starting my personal Bible study with the book of John in the New Testament. She gave me a commentary to help. It just shows how naïve I am about the Bible. I didn't even realize there were special books to help a person study.

After Easter I'll go to Bible study, and today I'll start reading John. Last night I went to the Lenten service. I'm getting to be quite a stirred-up Christian. I think that's better than the don't-bother-me-too-much Christian I was before. And I'm so thankful Daddy is eager to go to church too—even on Wednesdays. We often talk about the sermon on the way home. Mandy, I'm just beginning to find out how much was missing from my life.

Friday, March 11

Dearest Mandy,

I read the first chapter in John yesterday. Don't laugh, Mandy, because I only read one chapter; that chapter is long. And there was so much in it. I read the commentary too, so I'd really begin to understand what I was reading.

97

In the very first verse, I learned that Jesus was right there with the Father at creation. I'm sure I had probably heard that in my confirmation classes, but I didn't remember it. I got such a feeling of the holiness of God, of the eternity of him.

Then I read about John the Baptist. Did you know that his coming was predicted thousands of years before, just like the coming of Jesus was? It amazes me how God plans things so far ahead of time and then waits patiently for them to happen. It's as though he's already written the book of this earth, so of course he knows what's going to happen next.

I read about Jesus calling his disciples. I can't imagine Jesus saying "Follow me!" and dropping everything to go after him. I'm more like Nathanael, who needed convincing. I wish I were like the two disciples who just followed him without asking questions, but in my heart, I am like Nathanael. I think that's okay. After all, he told Jesus, "You are the Son of God; you are the King of Israel." It just takes longer for some of us.

Saturday, March 12

Dearest Mandy,

I told Daddy about my Bible reading yesterday, and he's going to read John too. He'll read it at night before he starts his school work. Then we can discuss it at dinner the next night. I have a feeling mealtimes will be getting longer.

Here I am, back again. And you didn't even know I was gone. The phone rang, and guess what! Aunt Betina had her baby 30 minutes ago! Jennifer Mandy made her appearance at 8:31 A.M., weighing 6 pounds, 3 ounces, and measuring 18 inches long. Kind of teeny, but Uncle Jeff said she has good lungs and is doing well. It's amazing that it was a Saturday when we thought Aunt Betina might lose the baby and a Saturday when her baby was born. Aunt Betina is fine too. Uncle Jeff said she's so happy and excited that she can't stop crying. Oh, how I wish we could be there! God did answer our prayers for a healthy baby. Peg told me God always answers prayer. Sometimes his answer is no.

Sunday, March 13

Dearest Mandy,

Daddy and I spent a long time talking to Uncle Jeff and Aunt Betina. Uncle Jeff thinks Jennifer looks just like her mommy with the same dark eyes and hair. They're planning her baptism for Easter Sunday. Isn't that a wonderful day for a baptism? We think about Jesus raised from the dead, and then we see a baby born again.

Easter works well for us. Daddy has off from Thursday, the 24th, through Easter Monday. It's over 8 hours to Uncle Jeff and Aunt Betina's, so it's quite a trip. We'll go as far as Grandma and Grandpa Jurgens, stay overnight there on Wednesday, and then take them along the next day. Stan said we could use their van so we won't be so crowded. Then we can take the baby stuff too. I worry about using someone else's vehicle, but Peg and Stan don't seem too concerned about it.

Oh, Mandy, I am so excited! Aunt Betina and Uncle Jeff have asked us to be godparents. I've already asked God to keep Jennifer safe and to help us be good sponsors to this baby. I know she's in his hands.

Dearest Mandy,

Peg and I went shopping today for a baptismal gift. I found a beautiful silver picture frame that says "God's Special Blessing" on it. Isn't that perfect? Then I bought a tiny cross almost like the one they gave you for your baptism. Of course, I had to shop for a pretty dress too. I found a lacy pink one with rosebuds embroidered on the bodice. Thank goodness it was on sale or I'd never have been able to afford it. With her dark hair, I'm sure Jennifer will be beautiful in it.

There's something bittersweet in all this, my love, but there's real joy too. It's strange, I never knew what sorrow was until I lost you, but I'm not sure I knew true joy either. I thought you were my joy, but I've learned that joy is more than happiness. It's a state of the heart that doesn't depend on the circumstances of life. I haven't gotten it all together yet, at least not in the completely accepting, quiet way Peg has, but my spirit is beginning to understand, even if my mind still sometimes struggles.

Tuesday, March 15

Dearest Mandy,

I called Nana and Uncle Steve last night to tell them about our new little niece. Nana was a bit apprehensive. "Are you doing all right with it?" she asked. I laughed and said I was doing just fine.

I want Aunt Betina and Uncle Jeff to be happy, and I'm glad for them. I wrote down a passage one day when I was rummaging through the Bible, before Peg told me to start with John. It was Romans 12:15: "Rejoice with those who rejoice; mourn with those who mourn." At the time I was thinking of all the people who mourned with us when you went home, but today I'm thinking about rejoicing. They're kind of the same in a way, aren't they, Mandy? They both say "I care," but we have to be careful not to confuse the two. If I mourn while Aunt Betina and Uncle Jeff rejoice, it dims their joy. I remember when thoughtless people made light of your loss because you were so young. "It's not like losing a child you've had for years," one elderly woman told me. "You didn't have much time to get attached to her. Besides, you know she's in heaven. " I felt like she was telling me I should rejoice when my heart needed to mourn. I hope I never get the two confused.

Wednesday, March 16

Dearest Mandy,

Daddy and I didn't get to our *John discussion* tonight because we had church. I can't believe Easter's almost here. I'll miss going to these Lenten services. It's strange that I should say that since I never went other years. Now they've become important to Daddy and me. Nana's been going to her church's Lenten services too, and she said she was sorry we never did that enough as a family when Uncle Steve and I were growing up. Looks like God used you to move us in his direction, doesn't it? Uncle Steve always goes to Lenten services, no matter how busy he is. When I called him the other night, he asked if Daddy and I were going. He's encouraged us to do that, but we never listened to him before. It's not that Uncle Steve hasn't tried to gently push us toward God all these years. We'd just gotten way too good at pushing back.

Dearest Mandy,

It's overcast today. I watched the weather at noon, and they're predicting a major snowstorm tonight and tomorrow. I love snow, but I don't want winter anymore. Oh well, it would be far worse to get a snowstorm when we're traveling to Uncle Jeff and Aunt Betina's. Maybe Daddy won't have school tomorrow. Then we can move the bookshelves into his study and get that room straightened out. Maybe I'll put another page into your scrapbook too. That's the perfect job for a snowy day.

Last night Pastor talked about the punishment Jesus suffered. "By his stripes we are healed," the Bible says. Pastor said Jesus was speaking about the sin that "sickens" and eventually kills us. Because Jesus came, however, death is only temporary. Just think, if Jesus hadn't come, there wouldn't be any heaven or eternal life. Then my tears would never stop, my crying would never cease. I'd have no hope of ever seeing you again, and that would be even sadder than the day you left.

Friday, March 18

Dearest Mandy,

The weatherman was right: snow, snow, and more snow. Daddy didn't have school, so this morning we got those shelves in place and filled them up. It looks so much better in the study now. And it was nice to work with Daddy. We haven't had a chance to work together on anything since we cleaned out your room.

I'm exhausted tonight. That's because after the storm ended this afternoon, we went out and cleared the snow.

That wasn't so bad, but then Daddy threw a snowball at me. I threw one back. He ran after me into the backyard, and we had an all-out snowball fight, ducking behind trees, hiding next to the garage, sneaking up on each other until WHOMP! One of us got it in the back. Finally, Daddy grabbed me and pulled me down into a pile of snow. We wrestled for a while, and then he suddenly held me down and kissed me, long and warm and wonderful. I hope Peg wasn't watching out her window.

Saturday, March 19

Dearest Mandy,

Daddy tromped through the snow to work with Stan again, so I called Peg and asked if she'd like to come and do some scrapbooking with me. I never did get to it yesterday.

Peg lugged her stuff over, I made coffee, and we worked and chatted. "Looks as though you and Dave enjoyed the snow yesterday," she remarked offhandedly. Did I detect a twinkle in her eye? I blushed and smiled. How much did she see, I wondered.

"It would be nice if Stan chased me once in a while like that," Peg said with a laugh, "but he'd probably put his back out!"

Peg surprises me. I guess I always thought devoted Christians like Peg and Stan wouldn't have a sense of humor, but those two have proved me wrong. I told Peg that, and she almost choked on her coffee. "Why," she said, "I believe God has a sense of humor too. Remember the feeding of the five thousand? When the disciples were concerned about the crowd being hungry, Jesus told them, 'You give them something to eat.' I think he must have said that with a smile on his face."

Peg makes me look at God in ways I never did before. I like getting to know him through her eyes.

Sunday, March 20

Dearest Mandy,

It's Palm Sunday, and we plowed through piles of slushy snow to get to church. At least at this time of year it melts quickly. The service marked the confirmation of a class full of young people. I don't know any of the confirmands, but they all looked nervous. I remember how scared I was on my confirmation day. I remember promising God that I would suffer anything, even death, rather than fall away from him. I haven't kept that promise very well. I wonder what made me forget it, and I wonder what brought it back to mind after all these years.

Monday, March 21

Dearest Mandy,

In a few short days we'll be on our way to Aunt Betina and Uncle Jeff's. I went through the dresser in your room (we left it in there for guests) and tried to sort out clothes for your new cousin. I put your underwear, booties, and onesies in a box to store. Most of those are somewhat stained, and I'm sure Aunt Betina will get nice new things like that. I did put that pink dress from Uncle Steve and a few of my favorite outfits in your cousin's bag. Even if we have another girl someday, I won't be able to look at her in those clothes without thinking of you. And I had some brand new wintry clothes that you never got to wear. It's all going to Jennifer.

Yes, Mandy, I cried a bit, but there was peace too, knowing that I could at last fold those clothes, put them into the bag, and give them away. Part of me let go of you this afternoon, and the tears I shed were tears of fond remembrances, not bitterness. There is a difference.

Dearest Mandy,

I can't believe how quickly the snow disappeared. I went for a walk today, and for the most part, the sidewalks were clear. It was a bit humid, but that only made the promise of spring more evident. Daffodils bloomed everywhere like small rays of sunshine. Maybe I'll plant bulbs this fall so we have some beauty to jump-start the season next year. I'll call it "Mandy's Garden," and it will remind me of your cheery disposition and heart-catching smile. Your life was a pledge, Mandy, a promise of a summer to follow the spring, a promise God never kept. No, that's not right. God did keep his promise, but not in my flower bed. Instead, you bloom forever in the eternal summertime of heaven.

Dearest Mandy,

We're leaving this afternoon when Daddy gets home from school, so I don't have much time to write. I have to pack and get things in order before we leave. The Tomelsons brought their van over last night, and we got all the baby stuff for Jennifer stowed away. It's a four-hour trip to Grandma and Grandpa Jurgens and another five hours from there to Uncle Jeff's. Staying overnight with Grandma and Grandpa will help. It'll be nice traveling with them. We don't get to see them as often as we should. Grandma

Jurgens crocheted a mint-green and light yellow blanket for Jennifer. It sounds so pretty. Those grandmas and grandpas are pretty special, aren't they, Mandy? You certainly seemed to love your "grand" people, and they loved you too. I'm happy that Grandma and Grandpa Jurgens get another chance to enjoy a baby. Maybe someday Nana will too.

Maundy Thursday, March 24

Dearest Mandy,

I'm tired tonight. It's been a long two days. We got to Grandma and Grandpa's about nine last night, talked a while, and went to bed. We were up by six and in the van before seven. (You know how motivated Daddy is when he's on the road.) We got to Uncle Jeff and Aunt Betina's a little after noon. We'd told Aunt Betina not to plan lunch, so Grandma and Grandpa treated us all at a local sandwich shop. We spent the afternoon visiting, holding Jennifer, opening presents, etc.

Tonight we went to the Maundy Thursday service. It seemed strange to go to communion at a different church, but it was wonderful to share that Supper with family. I've always loved going to communion on Maundy Thursday, but I don't think I ever appreciated it before as much as I did this year. The words "poured out for you for the forgiveness of sins" touched my heart. I have so many sins to forgive, Mandy. My anger, my bitterness—I've held on to them much too long. I need to give them to Jesus and let him carry them to the cross.

Dearest Mandy,

I'll bet you thought I wasn't going to tell you about your little cousin, didn't you? I was so tired last night that I decided to wait and write about her today. Oh, Sweetie, she is beautiful! She has a head of pitch-black hair that curls into tiny commas. She got the color from Aunt Betina, but the curls come from Uncle Jeff. Your hair was even curlier, like Daddy's, but you got the blondness from me. Babies are always such a wonderful surprise; you never know quite what to expect until they're here and you can see how God put them together. I do think she looks like Aunt Betina, but she has Uncle Jeff's turned-up nose. (He hates his nose.)

Aunt Betina said Jenny is a good baby, and she hasn't even fussed much at night. I remember being tired all the time when we brought you home. You had a hard time learning to sleep through the night. "I do worry sometimes," Aunt Betina said. "I wake up in the darkness and listen to the quiet, and my heart starts to pound. Then I go check, and Jenny's sleeping peacefully. I pray to the Lord to keep her safe and put her into his hands. It's the only way I can get back to sleep."

Poor Aunt Betina! Your sudden leaving upset her more than I knew. I don't know if any of us will ever feel secure with a baby again. I'm sorry about that, and I'm sorry it has to shadow the joy of a new child. Perhaps God wants us all to value life more. He must want us to look more to him, as Aunt Betina is, and place our precious gifts into his caring hands. I prayed for you too, Mandy, but I know now my prayers were selfish. When I asked God to take care of you, I was only thinking of Daddy and me and how you belonged to us and nothing could take you away. In the last few weeks, I've thought often about those prayers. In his own way, God did answer them. He took care of you, my dearest child. He took you to heaven, where you'll never know pain or sadness. You'll never be hungry or thirsty, and you'll never suffer the troubles of earthly life. I am comforted by knowing you have eternal joy in Jesus' arms.

Saturday, March 26

Dearest Mandy,

Last night, Good Friday, I sat in a pew and thought about death and pain and sorrow. That wasn't hard for me to do; I've had a lot of practice. I thought of God giving up his only Son for me, and it was all I could do to keep from crying. I don't deserve that kind of love. None of us do. The service, the sermon, the caring people—they all touched my heart. I went back to the house saddened to think of Jesus on that cross, yet quieted and uplifted in my spirit. Maybe that's because I know the rest of the story—I know about the resurrection.

I've been a bit into my own thoughts lately, haven't I? I told Peg about that, and she said it's all part of my healing—that we have to turn over every stone of our lives until we make peace through it all. "And the Holy Spirit helps," she added, just like she was talking about a close friend. Well, to Peg, God is a close friend. I still don't know him as well as she does, but I think we're almost on a first-name basis now. He is awfully hard to get to know, Mandy. I've learned I can't invent God to my liking. I can't always understand him. And I certainly can't control him. It's scary to think I really can't control anything in my life. Peg says life gets much easier when we just let God be in charge. I've been trying to do that. But too often I still want to do things my way. It's like falling backward and trusting someone to catch you. I never could do that either.

Easter Sunday, March 27

Dearest Mandy,

What a glorious day it was today! The sun was shining, and it was almost warm. Actually, it wasn't bad at all, considering how early Easter is this year. The church was filled for the late service. And, of course, Easter Sunday was just the perfect day for Jennifer's baptism. How good it felt to hold a baby again! I willed myself not to cry—not to even get teary-eyed. I told myself this was a different time and place, a different child; but, oh, that tiny bit of life felt so much like you in my arms.

Jennifer slept through the entire service, including her baptism. When you were baptized, Daddy and I didn't take it as seriously as we did today. It was a rite I knew was performed, but I'd never thought much about what it meant, not until we lost you. Even when Uncle Steve talked to Daddy and me beforehand and explained the promise of faith that Baptism gives, I hardly listened. I just thought Uncle Steve was being his usual religious self again. Now I know he loved us and wanted desperately for us to grow in spirit, to truly see with eyes of faith what Baptism was working in you. I wish I'd paid closer attention.

After church we had a Baptism/Easter dinner in the church hall. Since Thursday Grandma, Aunt Betina, and I had worked on side dishes and desserts to go with the ham. (Don't worry, Mandy, we didn't let Aunt Betina do too much.) Aunt Betina's parents came, and so did one of her sisters and her husband, so we had a nice group. I was thrilled to share this day with Jennifer, and Daddy and I will work diligently to be good godparents. We know now how fragile life is, and even little children need to learn about their Savior.

Dearest Mandy,

We made the long trip back in one day. At least we had more than one driver, so that helped. I dozed a little during the ride, but I was still exhausted when we got home. Driving always makes me tired. We got everything into the house, but I haven't unpacked yet. I'll do that tomorrow. Tonight I'm going straight to bed.

Dearest Mandy,

I can't believe Easter is over, the baptism is over, the trip is over. I unpacked this morning, but didn't do much else. I guess I'm still tired from our busy holiday. Daddy seemed pretty perky this morning. He's always ready to go back to school. I'm glad he enjoys his job, even if he doesn't always enjoy all the extras that go with it. I wish I could find something that would satisfy me. I honestly don't know what I'm looking for. Peg would say to pray about it. I want to do my Bible reading yet, and then I *will* pray about it.

Dearest Mandy,

Peg came over this morning, and we had one of our long talks. I told her all about the baptism, all about Jennifer. She asked how I got through everything, and I could honestly say it wasn't as bad as I thought it would be. I said that even giving away your clothes and sharing your things wasn't too painful, especially when I saw how grateful Aunt Betina and Uncle Jeff were.

Peg nodded. "You're learning to let go, Carrie," she said. "That doesn't mean forgetting. It just means putting the past into the past and trusting God for the future."

I soak up Peg's words, Mandy; I soak them up and let them seep all through me. They give me the direction I need. When Peg speaks I know her thoughts are coming straight out of God's Word, and they always help me focus my spirit. I pray that someday I can help someone the way Peg has helped me. But I sure have a lot of growing to do before I have a faith as strong as hers.

Thursday, March 31

Dearest Mandy,

Today was our first Bible study on the book of Job. Peg was right, our teacher is fantastic. I was a bit scared because I've never gone to a Bible study before. I'm ashamed to say that, now that I know that a person like me can't get through life on her own. I need to find God, to lean on him to lead my life. That doesn't come easily, but it's a lot easier than trying to live without him. I know I've been trying to do that for over a year, and all it got me was more anger, more bitterness, more depression.

Peg told me there was no reason to be afraid; some of the women there were first-timers just like me. Today Pat just presented an overview of Job so we'd get to know him better. She said some people don't think Job really happened; they think that book of the Bible is just a symbolic story about God's care. Pat shared that Job is, of course, an inspired writing. She seemed to be looking right at me when she said, "Any of you who have gone through difficult times will know after studying Job that what he went through is true." I'm eager to find out exactly what Pat means by that.

Dearest Mandy,

It's the first of April already! I remember when I was teaching and all the kids would tell outlandish stories and then yell, "April Fool!" I got really tired of it by the end of the day. Sometimes I wish I could walk into your nursery, see you cooing in your bed, and someone would yell, "April Fool!" and you wouldn't be dead at all.

Even though I'm feeling better, and I'm slowly learning to deal with losing you, the emptiness is still there. I still see you in my dreams, but you're so far away, and I can't get to you. My feet won't move, and I turn wrong corners. I can't find you, and a terrible fear grips me. Sometimes I hear a shadowy voice whispering, "She's gone; she's gone." I wake up with my heart pounding, and I realize for the millionth time that you really are gone. The shock of losing you never seems to go away completely. When I'm old and wrinkled, will I still see you in my dreams? Will I still hear you, even if there's a new baby crying in the darkness?

Daddy said he still thinks about you too. It seems to quiet both of us to visit your tiny grave. I know you're not there, but seeing your name on that tombstone assures me that you were real, that you came and lived, and filled our lives with joy. I want to remember those times, and yet I struggle to forget.

Dearest Mandy,

Daddy finished the rocking horse today, and it's so beautiful. He even stained it himself. It isn't very big, so it should be just the right size for Jennifer's first birthday.

Daddy told me he planned to finish sooner, but sometimes he and Stan got busy talking, and he'd forget to work. I'm glad Stan makes time for Daddy. He knows how to ease Daddy's heart, just as Peg knows how to ease mine.

I used to think I was such an all-together person, Mandy. Then you left, and my life became a Tilt-a-Whirl and a roller coaster all in one. I guess I wasn't as grounded as I thought, probably because I'd left God pretty much out of the equation. Daddy and I are learning that life isn't life without him.

Sunday, April 3

Dearest Mandy,

Peg and Stan went with Daddy and me for dinner after church today. I made a chocolate jelly roll yesterday, so they came over afterward for dessert. (Yes, my love for cooking really is coming back.) We just sat around and talked. It was a pleasant, relaxed afternoon. I'm amazed that the difference in our ages means so little. It helps to have our faith in common.

Peg asked if I'd done any more scrapbooking lately. I told her I hadn't done much. I seem to work better when we do it together. She said there was a sale next week at the little place downtown where I got my other stuff. We looked through your pictures and jotted down ideas for backgrounds, stickers, etc. I don't want to spend money on things I can't use. Peg loved the picture of you next to Uncle Steve's pink teddy bear. You remember that picture. You had just learned to hold up your head. We laid you on your tummy and Daddy played peek-a-boo to make you laugh. You giggled so much that you got the hiccups. During one big giggle, I snapped the camera at just the right time. It's always been my favorite "homemade" picture. We made lots of copies. Peg asked if she could have one. That gladdened my heart. I love to share you with others.

Monday, April 4

Dearest Mandy,

Peg came over this afternoon; I didn't expect to see her again so soon. She said she'd been thinking about me all morning, and one thing was bothering her. I laughed and asked, "Only one thing?" (I feel like there are so many loose ends in my life.)

She laughed too. "You're such a nice person, Carrie," she said, "so caring, so easy to talk to. Yet I never hear you talk about any friends. Surely you've acquired friends over the years. They would be a help to you in recovering from Mandy's loss."

I felt my cheeks getting red. "Yes, I do, . . . *did* have friends," I told her. "But I stopped e-mailing them because I couldn't bear to hear about their happy lives. That was pretty selfish, wasn't it?"

"Yes," Peg said, "but it was also survival. But I think now you're ready to move on. Do you still have their e-mail addresses? No time like the present to renew old acquaintances."

We spent the rest of the afternoon e-mailing my friends. It's been so long since I did anything on the computer that Peg had to refresh me. I guess because the computer is in Daddy's study, I just never think to use it. Even when I taught, I only knew the basics. Peg said she's going to enroll me in a computer course. She'll make a functioning human being of me yet!

115

of my endless days. At
the house is still, your spi

Tuesday, April 5

Dearest Mandy,

I was eager to check my e-mail today. Actually, Daddy
and I share an address, so I guess it's our e-mail, although
I don't think Daddy will want to be in on my "friendship
circle." I wrote six friends. Two already answered, and one
came back as undeliverable. Then I remembered that Emily
sent a new e-mail address in her Christmas letter. I found
it later and wrote her again at the new address. I hope it
goes through.

Stacey and Janna, the two friends who answered, were
so kind. Peg helped me write their e-mails yesterday. I told
them honestly why I hadn't written, apologized, and said
I was getting better and needed their friendship. Both of
them were understanding. Stacey told me I'd been in her
prayers every day. She had sent me several cards and notes
besides her e-mails, and I had never answered any of them.
She even called me once, but I was pretty distant. Why
have I been so hard on a friend who only tried to help me?
I guess I was so twisted into my own ball of grief that I
couldn't relate to anyone or anything. Stacey was worried
about me and relieved to hear I was getting better. I'd
forgotten how good it felt to share with friends. Peg is
right; I need them.

Peg thought maybe I could call one of my fellow
teachers from school and visit with her, but I nixed that. I
never did feel comfortable with that group. All of them
were older than me, and they treated me like a youngster.
They laughed at my ideas and said I worked too hard. They
gave us that big stroller when you were born, Mandy. And
I got lots of cards and a lovely bouquet when God took
you home. But no one ever called after that, and no one
ever asked how I was doing if we met on the street. I'll be
kind and say they were at a loss for words, but part of me
wonders if they really cared.

Dearest Mandy,

Peg and I went to the scrapbook sale today. I tried not to buy much, but it was hard. I did find a book of baby papers to use for backgrounds. I invested in stickers too, but that's all. Pretty soon Daddy will tell me I better get a job if I want an expensive hobby. I can't wait till I have all your pictures in my book. It will be a permanent remembrance of you. If God gives us other children, I can show them the scrapbook and tell them, "This is the baby God called home when she was only four-and-a-half months old. Her name is Mandy." See, my dearest, you won't be forgotten.

Thursday, April 7

Dearest Mandy,

I keep forgetting to tell you, Daddy and I are slowly working our way through the book of John. Peg was right about it being a good place to start learning about God. I feel like I'm getting to know Jesus better every day. Daddy and I are only on chapter 10, although we began our study quite a while ago. Some nights he has to hurry to a meeting, and we can't discuss it. Then there was Easter, which took away some time. And sometimes we spend more than one night on a chapter. We spent three whole evenings on Jesus' meeting with Nicodemus! Wouldn't it be wonderful to be Nicodemus and sit at Jesus' feet? "You must be born again." Those words play often through my mind. I was baptized as a baby, and I've been a Christian all my life, yet I feel as though in some way, I too am being "reborn." I was an ugly caterpillar, but through the Holy Spirit working in me, I'm slowly becoming a butterfly. I know it has to be the Holy Spirit. Nothing touched my sorrow all those months and months I grieved for you. Yet, when Peg brought God's Word to me, the pain inside me began to lessen, and my life has been changing ever since.

Friday, April 8

Dearest Mandy,

Peg and I went to Bible study yesterday, but we didn't even get through chapter 1 because so many people asked questions. No, Mandy, I didn't ask any yet. I'm still a bit shy, but it made me feel better to see that others had questions too. Did you know that Satan isn't really the devil's name, but his title? It means "The Adversary" or "Enemy of God." If the devil is God's enemy, I wonder if he's the one who plants the unrelenting sorrow and all the tears that keep us from seeing the hand of God in our lives. I started thinking about that and called Peg to see what she thought. She said, "Yes."

Saturday, April 9

Dearest Mandy,

I had Peg and Stan over for lunch today. They've done so much for us, and there's so little I can do to thank them. We sat and visited once lunch was over. Peg assured me that when she told me yesterday that Satan can rob our joy, she didn't mean that we shouldn't grieve. "After all," she said, "Jesus himself wept at the grave of Lazarus." I hadn't thought about that. I guess what's wrong is the kind of grieving that doesn't end, the kind that consumes us, the kind that doesn't point us to God. I was at that place, wasn't I, Mandy? I'm happy God loved me enough to send Peg and Pastor and Uncle Steve and all the other people who've helped me straighten out my life. Especially Peg.

Dearest Mandy,

Daddy told me we were going to late service today so he could take me out to dinner for my birthday. My birthday's not till Wednesday, but he's got a meeting that night. He took me to The Wishing Well, and I couldn't help but remember the last time we were there, in January, the night I got the old Daddy back. Daddy remembered too. He'd reserved a table—that one at the very back by the window that we had the last time we came. Wasn't that sweet of him? Today it was sunny, and the huge pots outside were abloom with hyacinths and tulips, all in shades of purple and pink.

They have a buffet on Sundays, and everything was great. When we finished eating, Daddy reached into his suit coat and pulled out a little box. "Sorry I didn't get it wrapped," he said sheepishly.

I opened it up, and there inside were heart earrings to match the necklace Daddy gave me at Christmas. "I couldn't afford both then," he explained. "I want them to remind you that you have my heart always, even when I'm a big dope and don't act like a husband should. Sometimes I'm just a slow learner."

"They're beautiful," I told him, "and so are you." It made me feel good to know that even at Christmas, when I felt our marriage was dissolving, Daddy did love me. The necklace was his way of saying what his words couldn't. He's getting better at expressing himself, and I'm getting better at understanding him. We just needed to meet halfway.

After dinner we stopped at the grocery store, and I bought a little pot of red tulips to put on your grave. I don't know how long they'll last out there, but I remembered how you reached for anything brightly colored. I know you'd have liked them.

119

They looked just the right size for your little grave and fit perfectly into the holder by your headstone. I read the engraving again, as I do every time I come, like it's the only way I can believe you're really gone. June 15 to October 25. Not a very long time for a life, but plenty long enough to break my heart.

Monday, April 11

Dearest Mandy,

I'm corresponding with a few of my friends via e-mail. They've been supportive and understanding. Not all my mail went through, so I think I'll write notes to those friends and see what happens. I'm certainly glad Peg helped me get back to Stacey and Janna and Emily.

Speaking of Peg, her aunt is visiting next week, although she hasn't said much about her. I think I'll have them over one day and get acquainted.

I talked to Nana last night. It was nice to hear the happiness back in her voice. Do you know what she's doing, Mandy? She's volunteering at a grade school as a kind of foster grandparent. The children even call her "Granny Simmons." "I don't have Mandy anymore," she told me, "but I can make a difference in another child's life." I'm proud of her.

I wish I could find that same direction for my life. Teach again? Maybe, but I don't feel that pull. I know what Peg would say: "Wait on the Lord." I'm trying to do that. Really, I am.

Tuesday, April 12

Dearest Mandy,

I worked in the yard today. I dug a flower bed under your bedroom window. Now I have to plant some bulbs this fall so they'll bloom next spring. Remember, I told you I was going to do that. And I'll get some colorful perennials for this summer. Only bright, happy flowers can bloom in Mandy's Garden. No weeds allowed. It'll remind me of happy times, your smiling face, light and color and joy, not darkness and death.

I weeded a few other beds too. I was going to take a walk after that, but I was just plain pooped. I must get into that routine again. It was easy to walk almost every day when you were here. I knew you loved the sunshine and the wind teasing through your golden curls. If I start walking again, is it all right if I talk to you sometimes, just like I used to? Maybe if I listen closely, I'll even hear you answer in the breeze that stirs the leaves or the music of a melancholy wind chime on a cloudy day.

Wednesday, April 13

Dearest Mandy,

Happy birthday to me! We got up early this morning so Daddy could take me to breakfast. I protested because he's already taken me out for dinner. "Just wait till you see what I expect for my birthday," he teased. His isn't until September, so I have plenty of time to think about it.

We went to the little cafe down the street. It's not an impressive place, but the food is good. I had an omelet, more than I could eat. Daddy helped me out. (He always does.) It was a beautiful way to start the day. I went home and baked myself a birthday cake—chocolate with pink frosting—just cause I felt like pink today. We'll have it for dinner. Then I called Peg and asked her if she'd like to come scrapbook for a while. I couldn't think of any nicer way to celebrate my birthday. She said she'd be glad to since she'd cleaned all morning, getting ready for her aunt, and needed a rest.

I better go get things ready for our session. Maybe I'll have to cut the cake a little early so Peg and I can celebrate. I guess I should save it for dinner, but since it's my birthday, I can do what I want.

Thursday, April 14

Dearest Mandy,

I had a nice birthday yesterday, although Peg chided me for not letting her know sooner. "I'd have gotten you a gift," she said.

"I know," I answered. "That's why I didn't tell you."

Uncle Steve called last night and Nana too. "Well," Uncle Steve said, "where do you want your life to be next year this time?"

"I'm not sure," I told him. "I want to get a job, but I'm not certain what I want to do. I don't want to go back to teaching."

"I'll keep you in my prayers," he said. "You're talented, Carrie. I know God has some special plan for you."

A year ago I would have told him that I wasn't too fond of God's plans, but now I feel differently. Life unfolds as God wills it, and there's something exciting about looking at each new day as an opportunity for growing in faith. It's an adventure in which you never know what's lurking around the corner. Sometimes it's good. Sometimes it's bad. But always God works through it for our good.

Friday, April 15

Dearest Mandy,

Tax day, but Daddy's been done for a long time already. He's not a last-minute person. I'm always thankful when it's over and everything's paid.

I neglected to tell you about Bible study yesterday. We finished chapter 1, and I was shamed by Job's testimony after he'd lost so much. The last verse said that Job didn't sin by charging God with doing wrong. I guessed I've sinned plenty because I've charged God more than once with messing up my life. I'm glad God forgives, or I'd have no hope at all. I never used to think about my sins, and they really didn't bother me much. It took losing you to see that sin filled my whole being and I couldn't be right with God.

Saturday, April 16

Dearest Mandy,

Daddy and I were going to work in the yard today, but it rained. That's okay; I think it's a bit early yet anyway. We might still get some frost. The grass is greening up nicely. The year you were born it rained and rained all spring. I kept telling myself that every green leaf brought you one day closer to being born. I was so eager for that day. Little did I know that those raindrops were a silent forerunner for my tears.

Sunday, April 17

Dearest Mandy,

I wrote in this journal early yesterday, before the mail came. We got a beautiful picture of Jennifer from Aunt Betina and Uncle Jeff. She does look like pretty Aunt Betina. Jenny was wearing the dress I bought her, and she was smiling. Yes, really! I know babies don't smile that early, at least not for people reasons. Aunt Betina said the smile was a fluke—probably gas; but they caught the picture at just the right moment. I will get a little frame for it and put it next to your picture on the shelf.

I wish they didn't live so far away. I was worried about being jealous of Aunt Betina's baby and now here I am, as proud an aunt (and godmother) as anyone ever saw. I'm growing, aren't I, Mandy?

Monday April 18

Dearest Mandy,

Peg's aunt arrived today. I saw her get out of the Tomelson's van. (They picked her up at the airport.) She's a large woman and walks with a cane. I hope Peg and Stan have a good visit with her. I won't bother them today, but I will invite them over this week.

The sun's out today, but the flower beds are still wet. I spent most of the afternoon with my e-mail. Stacey just found out she's pregnant with her first baby. She and Brian have been married five years and thought they couldn't have children, so this is a wonderful surprise. I hope my loss doesn't scare her. Most babies grow up just fine, but it's hard not to worry. It will be difficult for me if God gives us another baby too. Peg says that's why I have to learn to let go, so I don't spend my whole life afraid and anxious. Philippians 4:6 says we should not be anxious about anything. That whole passage is about God being near, about peace and rejoicing. Since Peg showed me that passage, I read it often to refresh my spirit.

Tuesday, April 19

Dearest Mandy,

I invited Peg and her Aunt Sophie to come over tomorrow for lunch. I spent the morning combing through cookbooks for something fun to make. I think I'll try Golden Chicken Bake with Lime-Pear Salad, Chunky Rolls, and Strawberry Cheesecake. It will be so much fun to cook for them. Excuse me for leaving so soon, but I want to go to the store and buy all my groceries. Poor Daddy! He'll only get the leftovers.

Wednesday, April 20

Dearest Mandy,

Well, I had Peg and her Aunt Sophie for lunch, and now I know why Peg never said much about her. She ate my beautiful lunch (Peg said it was) without a word of appreciation. In fact, all she talked about was how terrible her life has been since her husband died, how unfair that she lost him, how cruel God was, and on and on and on. I asked her when she'd lost her husband, and she said 30 years ago. Can you imagine that? She's spent 30 long years complaining until now she's a bitter old lady.

I don't want to get like that, Mandy. There's something soothing about hugging your anger and pain around you and shutting out the world, but that comfort is only an illusion that turns your spirit sour and dries up your soul. I think God wanted me to see what I could become if I continued to live without him. I will pray for Aunt Sophie. It's never too late for God to work miracles.

Thursday, April 21

Dearest Mandy,

Today was Bible study again. Pat asked if any of us had ever felt like Job, ever had a loss that was almost impossible to deal with. One lady, Lynn, shared that her husband walked out one day and left her with two small children. Peg nudged me, and I tentatively raised my hand. "My baby died when she was four months old," I told them. "Her name was Mandy, and for a long time all the joy went out of my life. I wasn't as faithful as Job. I hated God. Then he sent Peg into my life, and slowly the light seeped into my soul again." I grabbed Peg's hand and saw that she was crying just like I was. Pat had tears in her eyes too.

"You and Lynn have endured some difficult times," she said. "I know what it's like to lose a child. My first little boy was stillborn. No one spoke about it; that was considered a no-no back then. All these years I've buried that pain deep inside my heart. I think today is a good time to share it and to start to heal."

Oh, Mandy, that opened up everything. More women shared, including Peg, and I discovered that God sends trials into many lives. For all of us that pain led us right there to that Bible study on Job. We didn't get very far in studying Job today, but the sharing was a learning and healing time too. I felt that for the first time, many of us dared to be vulnerable, dared to trust someone with the fragile pain of betrayal and loss. Even Pat, whom I never suspected of carrying such heartbreak, opened her soul.

Friday, April 22

Dearest Mandy,

I didn't sleep very well last night. Thoughts of the Bible study raced through my mind, and I lay there wide awake, trying to grasp the enormity of God's involvement in our lives. He touched each woman differently, yet we all agreed that his touching was the beginning of a new relationship with him. "Our trials are tailor-made for us," Pat said. "God knows the exact experience we need to reawaken us to his voice."

His voice. Did I ever really hear it before? Now it tells me to rest and be at peace in him. I know he will lead me and show me the way I should go. I fell asleep at last, thinking of green meadows and still waters.

Saturday, April 23

Dearest Mandy,

At last the weather's turned warmer. Daddy and I cleaned out flower beds and trimmed the rose bushes. I planted hollyhocks, purple coneflowers, and coreopsis in your bed. Then we went for a walk—just the two of us—down past the highway and into the wooded area behind Sweeney's old house. The brook back there bubbled and gurgled over the rocks. We sat on a large boulder and talked about nothing important at all. It was one of the loveliest days of my life.

Sunday, April 24

Dearest Mandy,

Stan took Daddy fishing this afternoon. Daddy fished when he was a boy, but he hasn't had a chance to do that since. I saw a boat in the garage when the Tomelsons first moved in, but I didn't think much about it. Apparently Daddy and Stan did. "He said the first nice weekend we have, he's going to take me out," Daddy told me. "I can use his gear for now. Maybe I'll have to get some of my own stuff if we go more often this summer."

A man from church told Stan he could fish on his private pond. Daddy will have a great time, and it's good for him to get away. At home he just works on school stuff or reads more history books, . . . and he's already a walking encyclopedia.

Peg invited me over to scrapbook. It won't be long and all your pictures will be in my album, ready to show anyone who wants to see them. Maybe then I'll have to start a new album of Daddy's fishing pictures.

Monday, April 25

Dearest Mandy,

Daddy actually caught three fish yesterday, so you know what we're going to be having for dinner tonight. Daddy said they'd taste better fried in a cast-iron skillet over an open fire. Too bad. Daddy will have to take his fish in the kitchen, at the table, in a civilized manner. I think they'll taste delicious no matter where we eat them.

Tuesday, April 26

Dearest Mandy,

We called Grandma and Grandpa Jurgens last night after our fish dinner, which, by the way, was scrumptious. I guess fishing made Daddy think of home and growing up. We had a nice visit with them. They bemoaned the fact that they don't get to see Jenny enough, and they're excited because Aunt Betina and Uncle Jeff are coming next weekend and staying for four days. Uncle Jeff has some vacation days, and Aunt Betina decided to quit her job at the gas company and stay home with Jenny.

I know Aunt Betina will love spending time with the baby. I'm happy I stayed home with you. The memories we made are more valuable than money, and I'd never be able to forgive myself if I had worked and lost what precious little time we had together.

Dearest Mandy,

Peg stopped over with a bouquet of tulips. How nice of her! I don't have any bulbs blooming—not till next year when your little garden comes up. The flowers looked so pretty in the cut-glass vase we got as a wedding present.

Peg and I visited, and she shared some insights about her aunt. She hadn't said much when we scrapbooked Sunday, but today she told me that her aunt won't go to church, won't let go of her hurt, and really doesn't seem to want to get better. "How can she live like that?" I asked.

Peg shook her head. "If we keep God out, it's the devil's invitation to come in," Peg answered. "Aunt Sophie turned her pain into anger against God, and she's never gotten over it."

"That could have been me," I said. "I was that bitter and angry too."

"Maybe that's why I prayed so much for you and tried to help you," Peg told me. "I saw what happens if you turn away from God."

"Thank you for not giving up on me," I said, "even when I almost gave up on myself."

Thursday, April 28

Dearest Mandy,

Bible study day again. Between John and Job, I'm learning all kinds of things about faith and the way God works in our lives.

Today, near the end of class, Pat asked me to share a little about how my life changed after I lost you and how I came to have peace. I think I talked too long, but

I wanted them to know that we can rejoice again, no matter what we've gone through. Several of the ladies asked me questions, and sometimes I felt as though I was the leader instead of Pat. She didn't seem to mind but just stood in the background, listening, and even asking a few questions herself. I shared the verse from Ecclesiastes that Peg and Uncle Steve both gave me: "He has made everything beautiful in its time."

When you went home to heaven, I didn't think life would ever be beautiful again. I certainly didn't understand that verse when I first heard it. Now I know that as God weaves the fabric of our lives, sorrows add strength to the cloth and soften the bright colors of joy into jewel tones of faith.

Friday, April 29

Dearest Mandy,

Walked today. Read. Exercised. E-mailed. I need some summer clothes, so I might go into Bursten to see what I can find at the mall tomorrow. Maybe Peg would like to go along.

Saturday, April 30

Dearest Mandy,

Another month gone. How fast the days fly by! Peg and I went to the mall. Guess what Daddy and Stan did? Yup, went fishing!

I found some shorts and tops, and I know I spent too much. I simply must get a job to help out. Peg knows I worry about money. She tells me not to. "God knows what you need," she said. "With or without a job, he'll provide. But if it's a job you want, I'll pray for that for you."

Dearest Mandy,

After church Daddy and I grilled steaks outside. The supermarket had a fantastic meat sale last week. We ate at our garage-sale picnic table. Someday we'll have nice patio furniture, but this works for now. Stan and Peg came over just as we were finishing and brought homemade ice cream for dessert. What a treat!

Peg and Stan couldn't stay long since they had plans for the afternoon. Daddy and I went for a walk after they left. (We had to wear off that ice cream!) We talked about our upcoming summer. We might drive to Nana's and hope Uncle Steve will meet us there. And we must get to see Aunt Betina, Uncle Jeff, and Jenny again. Babies grow up quickly, and I'm missing so much of her life.

Dearest Mandy,

Another rainy day! I decided to try my hand at the Internet. It wasn't too difficult to *navigate*. (Daddy says that, so I guess that's the proper language.) Daddy's shown me once or twice, but when I was depressed, I never cared about trying it. Today I decided to look up "SIDS" to see what I could find. Mandy, there are so many sites. Daddy got information for me right after you died. That's how I knew I did all the right things that should have protected you from SIDS. I found lots more information, but what interested me most were the many Web sites where people who'd lost children shared their feelings.

My heart broke for them because I knew what they were going through. Some of the children died longer ago than you did, and their parents were still lost in grief. Some had found their way past the suffocating depression and were beginning to heal. I felt such a kinship with each one of them. We belong to an exclusive club whose dues are loss and tears and a life that will never be the same.

Tuesday, May 3

Dearest Mandy,

I shared what I'd found on the Web sites with Daddy. I told him most of the stories were from women; I guess women just have to share to heal. "I wish I had understood that earlier," Daddy said.

Isn't it strange how we all grieve differently? And when we're grieving, it's hard to help someone else. You're all folded up in your own little cocoon and can't even think how to reach into someone else's life. Just the fact that I shared with Daddy shows how far we've both come. Only a few months ago I'd been afraid to tell him those stories, and he wouldn't have known what to say.

Wednesday, May 4

Dearest Mandy,

I don't know where the day went. I cleaned, did a little scrapbooking, then settled down with my recipe books to plan next week's meals. I used to do that all the time before you left, but then the darkness stole my ambition, as well as my joy. It took me a long time because I wanted to make things Daddy likes and try new recipes too. I think that fast track to his heart through his stomach is back in working order again.

Dearest Mandy,

Walked today, then sat in the park and listened to the birds. I watched one busy couple building a nest in the gutter on the main park building. I was so fascinated that I lost all track of time. Now I have to hurry and get dinner or my well-planned meal will be for naught. I made Daddy an angel food cake this morning after Bible class; it's his favorite! We'll have it with strawberries and cream. (Oh, all right, Cool Whip.)

Dearest Mandy,

Not much time to write today. I need to get groceries and stop by the scrapbook shop to see if I can find some summer stickers for your book. Then I want to e-mail Stacey and see how she's doing. And I just might sneak a peak at some of the SIDS sites I visited the other day.

Toodle-oo, Darling! Your mommy is one busy lady.

Dearest Mandy,

Did you notice that I didn't write you yesterday? That's because Daddy thought it would be fun to check out some farm auctions, and nothing else got done. We didn't find much, except what I would call *junk.* We did buy an old, sturdy dresser that needs to be refinished. (Guess who gets that job.) The guest room (your former nursery) has a cheap, rickety dresser that needs to be replaced. I think the dresser we bought will look nice in there once I get it done.

Isn't it funny? Pastor's sermon today was on "refinishing the old person." I wonder if he got his idea from farm auctions?

Monday, May 9

Dearest Mandy,

I worked on that dresser today. Daddy took it out of the garage and put it in the backyard for me before he went to school. What a job! I know it'll look nice when it's all finished, but today all I got done was taking off the old paint. I'm going to paint it white, I think. I'll keep it simple and maybe get some decorative knobs for it. I keep thinking what a pretty dresser it would make for a nursery. If I paint it white, I can always decorate it later for a baby.

Imagine that! I'm daring to think of babies again. Don't worry, my precious one. You'll always be close to my heart, and no one will ever take your place.

Tuesday, May 10

Dearest Mandy,

You won't believe what happened tonight. The phone rang about eight. It was Pastor, and he said he needed to talk to me. I couldn't imagine what he wanted. He told me he'd just come from visiting a member in the hospital who'd had a little boy. The baby only lived two hours, and the mother was having a hard time dealing with losing him. Pastor asked if I would go tomorrow and talk to her. "I tried to help her," he said, "but I think another woman, especially one who understands her pain, would be more effective. She's a fine Christian, Carrie, but this is pushing her faith to the limit. I knew you'd understand that."

I didn't know what to say. I feel so inadequate for a task like that, especially when I'm just rekindling my own faith. Then Peg's words came tumbling into my mind: Lean on God, Carrie. Trust him. I told Pastor that I'd visit Heather, but I would have to trust God for the right words. "I know that with his help, you'll do fine," he said. "We'll talk about your visit later."

So here I am, ready for bed, with my mind wide awake. Oh, Lord, give me the words to touch Heather's heart and help her through this trial.

Wednesday, May 11

Dearest Mandy,

It's hard for me to write tonight, my dearest Mandy. All the pain, all the awfulness of losing you came flooding back today when I visited Heather. I told her who I was and what had happened to you, and then I just held her, and we cried together.

"I'm glad you came," she said between sobs. "No one can understand how terrible this is unless they've gone through it."

I had no words of wisdom for her, no easy fix. I listened to her shattered hopes and dreams and felt the brokenness of her spirit. I couldn't tell her that someday it would be better, even though now I know it's true. I wasn't ready to hear that when I first lost you, and I know Heather wasn't ready either. I did tell her that God loved her, no matter how she felt right now. I begged her to cling to that, to know that even though God took Evan for his own reasons, God still loved her and grieved with her, just like he did at the grave of Lazarus. And I shared the words from Psalm 139:16 that began to heal me: "All the days ordained for me were written in your book before one of them came to be."

"Evan's ordained time was only two hours," I said. "You had only two hours to hold him and love him. Mandy's time was four months. Just like you, I thought it should be longer, but God decided their time on earth even before our babies were born. Mandy and Evan are the blessed ones, to be called so quickly back to heaven."

Heather told me Pastor came as soon as her husband, Jon, had called. And together they witnessed Evan being washed clean of sin through Baptism and committed into God's loving arms. How thankful I am that the Lord allowed them time for that!

I want to be there for Heather, Mandy. I'll call as soon as she gets home and then visit her. I won't let her go, just like Peg never let go of me. I'm not sure I'll always know how to help her, but I know Peg will support me too, and of course, God will always be there for me.

Thursday, May 12

Dearest Mandy,

I didn't say much at Bible study today, but I did a lot of listening. When I heard about Satan and God discussing their plans for Job, I wondered if the two of them had a similar conversation about me. I can almost hear Satan saying, "This will do her in. She's weak in her faith. She'll never make it through this trial, and Carrie will be mine, all mine."

I guess the devil didn't count on God . . . and Peg.

Friday, May 13

Dearest Mandy,

Heather went home today. I spent the afternoon with her. I've known her such a short time, and yet I feel as though our similar losses have made us soul mates. We talked about so many things. She seemed calmed to know that what she was feeling was normal after losing a child. She'd never had her faith tested before, and losing Evan sent her reeling. Yet, I see a strength in her that I lacked. She had a firm foundation of faith before she lost her baby, and that makes all the difference. Where I floundered, she's already treading water. I thought I was in charge of my universe. Heather, even in her sorrow, knows her world belongs to God.

Saturday, May 14

Dearest Mandy,

I called Peg today and told her about my visit with Heather last night. "Helping someone else will help your faith grow too, Carrie," she said. "I think God's plan for your life is beginning to unfold." I wasn't sure what she meant since I still often feel like I'm a blind person stumbling around in the dark. I don't know where I should go or what I should do. I'm so grateful our marriage is back on solid ground, and I'm thankful for getting to really know the Lord; but knowing his will for my life? I'm not certain about that. Oh well, Peg always seems to know where God's going way before I do.

Sunday, May 15

Dearest Mandy,

Daddy and I went for a long walk this afternoon. We held hands and remembered the May before you were born, how he'd make me walk to get some exercise, even though getting off the sofa with my watermelon stomach seemed exercise enough. "You always felt better once you walked, didn't you?" he asked.

I had to admit I did. It's funny, isn't it? Sometimes the things we don't want to do are the things that are best for us. I'd never have thought losing you would be good, but the changes God worked in me have certainly stretched and shaped my faith.

Monday, May 16

Dearest Mandy,

I think I have a touch of the flu today. I'll be back when I feel better.

Friday, May 20

Dearest Mandy,

Wow, I was gone a long time, wasn't I? I had more than a touch of the flu. I got a double whammy! I haven't been sick for such a long time, not even when I was most depressed over losing you.

Today Daddy's home sick. I know how terrible I felt, so I'm letting him do what I did all week—sleep, sleep, sleep.

Even without the flu, it's become harder and harder to write this journal. My days are full, and time is scarce. There's something else too: your haunting presence has quieted. The need to share with you has eased. Now when I'm hurting, I talk to God.

Saturday, May 21

Dearest Mandy,

I called Heather so she wouldn't think I'd forgotten her and made plans for her to come here next Tuesday. I'm still feeling droopy, but now I have a reason to get moving and get the house cleaned up. I sure didn't do anything last week.

Daddy's sick again today. I went to the store and bought a chicken so I could make some soup. I read somewhere that chicken soup really does help you get better. His stomach isn't reeling today, but he's still not moving much. Don't worry, I'll get him well again.

Sunday, May 22

Dearest Mandy,

I went to church alone today. It seemed strange to be there without Daddy. At least he's feeling somewhat better.

I was standing in the narthex talking to Peg and Stan after church when Pastor came and pulled me aside. "I need to talk to you about your visits with Heather," he said. "And I have something else I need to discuss with you too. Could you stop by my office after Bible class on Thursday? I was hoping to talk to you this week, but I didn't see you." I told him I'd been sick with the flu and assured him I'd stop in Thursday. I know he wanted to touch base about Heather, but whatever else could he want?

Monday, May 23

Dearest Mandy,

I cleaned today, made a chocolate cake for dinner, and answered e-mails. Now I have to call Nana and see how she's doing.

Tuesday, May 24

Dearest Mandy,

Heather came today, and Peg stopped in too. That was fine; I've wanted Heather to meet Peg. Heather's doing well, and she wants to scrapbook with us. She'd like to put her candid wedding pictures into an album. She asked if it would be okay to make a small album of her pregnancy pictures and put the few they took of Evan into a book too. Of course it would! There's something inside a mother that doesn't want her child to be forgotten, even if he only lived two hours.

Wednesday, May 25

Dearest Mandy,

Stan called Daddy last night and asked if he'd like to go fishing this weekend to celebrate the end of school. They're going to a private lake, so they won't have to hassle with the Memorial Day crowds, except on the road, of course. I wonder what I'll do.

Thursday, May 26

Dearest Mandy,

I had a hard time sitting through Bible class today, wondering what Pastor wanted to talk to me about. Usually I hang on every word, but today I was restless. It upsets me when I can't concentrate. I still have so much to learn about God.

I needn't have worried. Pastor had good news. First of all, he told me that he'd talked to Heather, and she was thankful for the help I'd given her. That made me happy. I've prayed a lot about Heather, and I know how fragile a person is when she's lost a child. I didn't want to hurt her more. Pastor assured me that I'd done fine. "In fact," he said, "I'd strongly recommend that you consider going into counseling, especially grief counseling. You have real gifts for that work, and your personal experience has been an asset for you."

I was shocked. I'd never thought about counseling before. I'll talk to Daddy about that when he comes home tonight. I'm not sure I'm ready for that; I'm really not sure about anything.

Friday, May 27

Dearest Mandy,

Last day of school for Daddy. Yippee! We went out for lunch at Burger Bob's to celebrate. Several of Daddy's students were in there too, so we didn't get much privacy. It's fun to watch Daddy interact with his students. I can tell they like him and respect him. And I know from the cards and notes we got that they hurt with him when you died.

I told Daddy what Pastor said. He was thoughtful when he answered. "Well, Carrie," he said, "you don't want to teach again, and counseling uses some of those same skills. We can look into it. I don't know what it will cost for you to go back to school."

Ah, there's the rub! I can't be spending money when I should be making money. I think counseling will be just that—a dream.

Saturday, May 28

Dearest Mandy,

Daddy and Stan are gone, and the house is so quiet.
Just a few months ago, on a day like this, I would hear
you in the silence. Now all I hear are the creaks and
groans of an aging house, and your voice is as silent as
the unused rocker in the living room. Funny, isn't it? When
you first left, I used to sit and rock there all the time, the
crick-crack, crick-crack of the old rocker comforting me
like a lullaby, the memory of you snuggled around my soul
like a soft blanket. I can't recapture that feeling. I'm not
even comfortable in that rocker now; it belongs to another
time, another place. It's a chair for mothering, and now I'm
a mother only in my heart.

Sunday, May 29

Dearest Mandy,

Daddy and Stan got skunked yesterday. Well, not
entirely. Daddy came home with a nasty sunburn, and
Stan didn't look much better. Peg and I scolded about
using sunscreen, but since Daddy and Stan both think
alike, they also both think they're invincible. Peg vowed
to apply the stuff herself to every visible part of Stan the
next time he goes fishing. I think she just might do it.

Monday, May 30

Dearest Mandy,

Peg invited us over for a Memorial Day picnic today.
"I guess we'll have to have burgers instead of fish," she

142

said. I'm bringing potato salad and an apple cake. We'll probably have enough food for an army. I want to ask Peg and Stan about the counseling idea. I haven't talked much to you about it, but it's always in the back of my mind. I don't know what to do. Maybe discussing it with objective people will help.

Tuesday, May 31

Dearest Mandy,

Well, Peg took my problem right into her hands. Or maybe I should say God's hands. "This is important to Carrie," she said. "Let's join hands and pray about it." So there we sat with the meat grilling and the food ready in the kitchen, with Peg asking God to help. "You know how fragile our faith often is," she told God, "and sometimes your will isn't easy to discern. Help Carrie find her way, to trust in you and find the guidance she needs."

Stan prayed too, thanking God for his blessing in giving us as neighbors and asking God to guide me. Then Daddy prayed and told God he loved me and wanted me to do whatever was best for our lives. That brought tears to my eyes. "Thank you for these friends gathered here," I continued, "and for my husband, who is a precious gift. Show me your will for my life."

I remembered the first time Peg prayed with me and how uncomfortable I was. When you know God is your best friend, prayer is much easier.

of my endless days. At n

the house is still, your spirit

Dearest Mandy,

June is here. I don't know where the year went. I feel like a lifetime has passed instead of just months. I love having Daddy home. We're working in the yard today, and then he's going to help me check Internet sites on grief counseling. I'm glad we're friends again. It would have been a long summer if we were still plodding along, bound in our separate chains of grief.

Dearest Mandy,

I took Heather along to Bible study today. She's read Job before, so she wasn't as lost as I'd be if I started late. I'm certainly glad God sent me better friends than Job had. He knew my faith was fragile and friends like Job's would have destroyed it. I wish I had his strength, but Peg says Job had some faltering times too. I guess that part is still coming.

Dearest Mandy,

Peg, Heather, and I scrapbooked today. Heather is doing a beautiful job with her wedding pictures. She went shopping last week and found the prettiest background papers. She said I could use some if I wanted. I'm just about done with your album, and I don't know what I'll do then. Maybe I'll use the doubles of the pictures I have and make a little scrapbook for Nana. She would love that.

Dearest Mandy,

I didn't even tell you yet what Daddy and I found on the Internet. Not much. That's probably why I forgot to mention it. Oh, there were sites, but none gave much information. The schools listed sounded like they might be schools over the Internet and others were too far away. I still don't know if I have to go through a whole counseling program or just take classes for grief counseling. And I'm not even sure I'm ready to go into counseling or if I really want to, to say nothing about paying for it. Peg says, as she always does, "Pray about it. God will answer." I must be too impatient. I've prayed every day, and no answers yet. I guess God has to remind me sometimes that my faith still needs sharpening.

Sunday, June 5

Dearest Mandy,

Pastor stopped me after church again. He asked me if I could come in and visit sometime this week. I'm going in tomorrow afternoon at one. I wonder what he wants this time?

Monday, June 6

Dearest Mandy,

Pastor and I had our visit this afternoon. Guess what, Mandy? He offered me a job! He said his secretary is overly busy since our congregation's grown, and he's gotten permission to hire someone part-time to help her. I would love to do that, but I do want to talk to Daddy first. It won't be a great income, but it might be a good way to get my feet wet in the working world again.

Pastor had more news for me. Pat, the woman who leads our Job Bible study, talked to him. It seems he shared with her that I'd helped someone who lost a child, and he was impressed with my work. Pat called him later and said she wanted to help me financially if I decided to go into grief counseling. She'd never told Pastor before that she'd lost a baby too. I knew Pat and her husband were well off. (Peg drove me past her gorgeous home one day.) But I never thought she'd want to help me. Pastor thought a job at the church would make it possible for me to work around classes. God does seem to have my life all figured out

Tuesday, June 7

Dearest Mandy,

I called Peg as soon as I finished writing you yesterday. She gave me her I-knew-God-would-answer-your-prayer laugh and asked what I was going to do. I told her I didn't know. "Don't rush into anything," Peg said. "Listen to other people, but don't let them decide what's best for you. Only God and you can do that."

I couldn't wait for Daddy to come home. "How does all this look to you?" he asked.

"I really would like to work at church," I told him. "But I'm still not sure about the counseling. I need to find out more about it."

"I think that job would be a wonderful opportunity," Daddy said, hugging me. "Pastor's secretary seems like a nice lady. I don't think you'll have a problem working with her."

How quickly life can change!

Dearest Mandy,

If there's one word to describe how I feel about all that's happening, it's *humble*. I'm not sure I have all the gifts Pastor thinks I have, and I'm even nervous about starting a new job. I feel like a person who's been sick a long time and needs to exercise her stiff muscles. My social and working skills feel pretty unused right now. Maybe job exercise will help.

Thursday, June 9

Dearest Mandy,

Today Job's words in chapter 9 seemed to be written just for me. Listen: "He performs wonders that cannot be fathomed, miracles that cannot be counted. When he passes me, I cannot see him; when he goes by, I cannot perceive him. If he snatches away, who can stop him? Who can say to him, 'What are you doing?'"

That's what I did for a long time: asked God what he was doing when he took you away. I had no right to do that, since God is God, and he can do what he wants. Yet, he loves me; and he's certainly done wonders and miracles in my life, even when I couldn't see him working.

Friday, June 10

Dearest Mandy,

I talked to Pat yesterday and thanked her for her generous offer. I also told her I wasn't sure about counseling. "That's okay," she said. "The offer's there if and when you

148

decide. I know how much I needed to talk to someone who understood when I lost my baby, and God put it into my heart to help you become a mentor to hurting moms."

I cried when I got home, Mandy. Why should God do so much for me when I've done so little for him? I don't know how he can love me, but he does, and he proves it every day.

Saturday, June 11

Dearest Mandy,

We went together with the Tomelsons to the lake today. Peg and I packed picnic lunches. We spent a lot of time on the water, cruising around in Stan's boat. It was a wonderful day. And, yes, we all put on sunscreen, although not without a bit of grousing from the men.

I am so tired tonight. Good-night, my sweet baby.

Sunday, June 12

Dearest Mandy,

Peg came over this afternoon with a beautifully wrapped gift. "What's this for?" I asked.

"It's for Mandy's birthday," she answered. I was taken aback. I know I told her a long time ago when your birthday was, but I didn't expect her to remember.

"We'll be visiting the kids and grandkids on Wednesday," Peg said, "so I'm giving you this early. I hope you like it."

I opened the card first. It had a cross on the front and a verse that talked about God leading us even when the way seemed dark. I couldn't imagine what Peg had gotten me. I tore off the pink-flowered paper and opened the flat,

149

square box. I drew my breath in sharply when I saw the exquisite counted cross-stitch inside a thin, gold frame. In pale green thread, the curved sides of a heart were formed by Daddy's name on one side and mine on the other. Inside the heart was the little picture of you I'd given Peg. Around your picture were pink roses and green vines. Underneath, your name was written in darker green thread.

"Oh, Peg," I told her, "it's beautiful. I'll treasure it always. I can't imagine how long it took you to make it!"

"It was a labor of love," she answered. "Whenever you look at Mandy's picture, remember what God has done in your life."

Monday, June 13

Dearest Mandy,

I've been thinking about Peg's words. It's amazing how losing you has touched so many people, not for the worse, as I thought it would, but for the better. Daddy and I know the Lord in a way we never did before, and our marriage is strengthened because of it. We became fast friends to Peg and Stan, our mentors. Nana has found a new purpose in life, and Uncle Steve found the goal he never had before. Grandma and Grandpa Jurgens show an increased love for God, and Aunt Betina and Uncle Jeff have learned to lean on him through every trial. I got to know Pastor better, I was able to minister to Heather, and there's a new job and opportunities awaiting me.

Oh, Mandy, my Mandy, God does make everything beautiful in his own good time.

Dearest Mandy,

Daddy has a meeting at church tomorrow night, so after dinner we went out to your grave. We had a prayer together as we stood over your tiny tombstone and committed the rest of our lives into God's keeping. I thanked God for the joy of you, the gift of you. Daddy blew his nose. "Good-bye, little Princess," he said. For both of us, the long journey to closure is almost over.

Wednesday, June 15

Dearest Mandy,

Today is your birthday. If you had lived, you would be two years old today, old enough to give hugs and kisses and fly into Daddy's arms when he came home from work. But God's ways aren't our ways, and his thoughts aren't our thoughts.

There will always be a quiet sadness in my heart that you stayed with us for so short a time. But surrounding that sadness is the joy of knowing God as my closest friend, my brother, my Lord, my Savior from eternal death.

I don't often feel you near me anymore, but today the sun is shining on the checkered tablecloth, filling me with the brightness of your presence. I know we will meet again, on that wonderful day when I too am free of this frail, sinful body.

I see that meeting so clearly now with my eyes of faith. You smile and wave in the loving arms of Jesus, eager for me to share the joys of heaven. The Savior puts you down, and now I am in his arms too, and all the pain, all the tears, all the emptiness is washed away forever.

Happy birthday, Mandy.